"OKAY, EVERYBODY ON THE CARPET," CHRIS SAID.

Chrissie felt a bit foolish sitting on the computer room carpet in the parking lot of her school. So, too, from the look of things, did Jessica and Henry. But they did as they were told. Kara, the dragon, snuggled happily around Chrissie's neck, apparently fast asleep and unbothered by what was happening.

Chris concentrated, sitting at the front of the carpet. *"To-chapa!" Be attached!* Chrissie felt some force like an invisible hand holding her in place. Jessica gave a squeal as she obviously felt the same effect. *"Maktar, to-fiva!" Carpet, fly!*

The carpet gave a shudder, then rippled underneath them. Jessica squealed again. Chrissie and the others rose from the ground, apparently held up by only the threads of a carpet. It wavered and shivered . . .

Then it shot into the sky so fast she almost screamed. . . .

So far their magic is working. But this is only the beginning of a dangerous mission where every second counts. . . .

The Magical States of America

Suddenly Twins!
Twice the Trouble!
Double Disaster! (coming March 2002)

Available from Minstrel Books
Published by Pocket Books

Twice the Trouble!

John Peel

A **MINSTREL**® BOOK

Published by POCKET BOOKS

New York   London   Toronto   Sydney   Singapore

13280482

This book is a work of fiction. Names, characters, places and incidents are products of the author's imagination or are used fictitiously. Any resemblance to actual events or locales or persons, living or dead, is entirely coincidental.

A MINSTREL PAPERBACK *Original*

 A Minstrel Book published by
POCKET BOOKS, a division of Simon & Schuster, Inc.
1230 Avenue of the Americas, New York, NY 10020

ISBN: 0-7434-1763-1

First Minstrel Books printing December 2001

10 9 8 7 6 5 4 3 2 1

A MINSTREL BOOK and colophon are registered trademarks of Simon & Schuster, Inc.

For information regarding special discounts for bulk purchases, please contact Simon & Schuster Special Sales at 1-800-456-6798 or business@simonandschuster.com

Cover art by John Gurney

Printed in the U.S.A.

This is for Jessica Sarah Peel

Twice the Trouble!

INTRODUCTION

Larry Lee looked out over the twinkling lights of the city of Dallas, Texas, and smiled to himself. Soon it—along with the rest of the world—would belong to him. He would become the very first King of the World. And it was all so very simple. People trusted him, and listened when he spoke. He knew he had a smooth tongue and a friendly manner that people loved. He caught sight of his features reflected back in the black nighttime glass and smiled some more. He looked good, too. Taking a comb from his pocket, he tidied up a stray wisp of his pure white hair and then straightened his neat white tie. He looked good in white, which was why he always wore it—even white shoes to match his many white suits.

The door to his office opened, and his assistant, Belmont, walked in. "Everything is ready," the man announced. "The space shuttle *Explorer* takes off in three hours."

"Perfect," Larry Lee said. "And once the shuttle is in orbit, there's nothing that anyone will be able to do to stop me. By this time tomorrow I shall rule the world."

"Yes, sir," Belmont said. "May I be the first to congratulate you?"

"Not until tomorrow," Larry Lee replied. "Let's not be too hasty. As King, I shall have to be very dignified." Then he grinned. "But until then I can gloat." He raised a triumphant fist into the air. "Yes! Perfect!"

Once those three hours were over, it would all be his. He looked out of the window again. Those poor, unsuspecting fools! The shuttle would launch at dawn. By supper he'd be in complete control of every aspect of their lives. . . .

chapter
ONE

Chrissie rolled over in bed and almost screamed. Then, as her heartbeat slowed to normal, she remembered everything that had happened. It was just so bizarre to be waking up with a dragon on your pillow.

Only a *small* dragon, of course, about the size of a ferret. Not as large as some of the ones Chrissie had seen in that strange mirror world to her own that she had visited. Some things in that world had been the reverse of what she considered normal. Instead of science, that world used magic. Instead of being a girl, in that world she was a boy named Chris. Her older brother, Sam, was a girl named Samantha. It had been very strange seeing things she knew turned on their heads.

She and Chris had teamed up to defeat an evil magician, Lori Lee, and save that other world from falling under her spell. That was when Samantha had given Kara, the dragon, to Chrissie. In that world everyone had a partner to help with magic.

The strangest thing was that Chrissie had been able to do magic in that world as well. Something about the air, the food, and the drink had brought magic into Chrissie's body. She'd been able to cast spells of her own. According to Kara, she'd be able to do that back in her own world, too, at least until the magic wore off. Then all she had to do was pop back through to the mirror world to renew it.

Which was incredibly cool, of course.

But sharing a pillow with a dragon—no matter how small and friendly—was definitely going to take some getting used to.

"Chrissie!" she heard her mom yell from downstairs. "Time to get up!"

"Okay, Mom!" she called back.

Kara opened one eye. "Please," she begged. "I'm a growing dragon. I need my rest. Don't yell so loudly."

Chrissie sighed. "Look, Kara, I thought we

had an agreement. You can't let anyone know you exist. Can't you hide somewhere, or something?"

"I'm comfy right here," the dragon answered. "I'm used to being treated nicely, you know." Her nose twitched. "Mmmm . . . Do I smell something cooking? I'm *starving*. I'll just pop down and—"

Chrissie grabbed Kara as the dragon launched herself at the door. "Aren't you *listening* to me?" she demanded. "You can't go down there and eat breakfast with my family. That's *not* keeping yourself hidden, is it?"

Kara gave a deep sigh. "You're trying to starve me to death, aren't you? You don't really love me, do you?" A large tear started forming in one of her eyes.

"It's not that at all," Chrissie said quickly. "I *do* love you. You're the most wonderful dragon in the world, really." That cheered Kara up again. "It's just that you're the *only* dragon in this world. If people found out about you . . . Well, I don't know exactly what would happen, but it wouldn't be good. People might want to experiment on you."

Kara sniffed. "The people on this world don't sound very nice."

"Most of them are okay," Chrissie said. "But there are some who would see you as a way to make money."

Kara shrugged, which made her long, green body shiver. "I can make money, anyway. You need some?"

"No!" How would she explain suddenly having a lot of cash? It was clear that Kara didn't get it. "Look, we'll go into this later. Right now I've got to get ready for school. You stay here, and I'll bring you some food up when I finish breakfast. Then you've got to stay hidden the rest of the day."

"All day?" The dragon jumped up to the windowsill and stuck her snout through the closed blinds. "It's a lovely day out there, and I don't know anything about this world of yours. I want to explore."

"Aren't you hearing *anything* I say?" Chrissie asked. "It's *dangerous* out there!"

"Pooh! How dangerous can it be? I'm the only dragon on the planet, so there's nothing out there that can hurt me." Then she screamed and jumped back, wrapping herself around Chrissie's neck and almost strangling her. "What's that monster?"

When Chrissie managed to breathe again,

she settled Kara back on the pillow. "That's not a monster, that's Daddy starting up his car. It always sounds a bit rough first thing in the morning. And if you ran in front of a car, dragon or no dragon, you'd be crushed to death. So do as I tell you, and *stay here!* I'm going to take a shower."

Chrissie wasn't certain she was doing the right thing leaving Kara alone, because Kara was still shaking from hearing the car start up. But Chrissie needed a shower. They didn't have cars on the other world—they had coaches pulled by unicorns. Quiet coaches. Chrissie wished she had a unicorn herself, but that would be even harder to hide than a pocket-size dragon.

The mirror in her bathroom stayed normal, only reflective glass, this morning. Yesterday she had seen Chris staring at her through it, right before he yanked her through into his world. Thankfully today she saw only herself looking back at her—blond hair, freckles, and all. She showered quickly, then dressed in jeans and a T-shirt for school. After slipping on her sneakers, she ran downstairs.

Mom, behind as always, had breakfast mostly ready. She was scanning the financial pages of the paper, sipping her coffee, when Chrissie grabbed her breakfast. She settled for oatmeal, but managed to snag a couple of strips of bacon from her brother Sam's plate before he appeared. He took after Mom, and was always a bit late for things. Chrissie wasn't certain what dragons ate, but she didn't think it would be oatmeal.

"Good morning, dear," Mom said, peering over the tops of her glasses, which were perched on the end of her nose and in danger of falling off, as usual.

"Hi, Mom. I'm gonna eat in my room. I've got to pack my backpack for school. See you!" Chrissie rushed off.

As she had hoped, Kara drooled over the bacon, then snarled and pounced on it. "I like to kill my own food," she explained. "But this is good." She crunched it down as Kara ate her oatmeal and fitted everything she needed into her backpack. Kara watched her with a distinct lack of interest. "So, what about drink?" the dragon asked. "I tried the big bowl in the other room, but I didn't like the smell of that blue water."

"That's the *toilet*," Chrissie explained, grossed out. "What do you like to drink?"

"Bitter fizz," Kara replied, licking her lips.

"Well, they don't make that on this world. Is water okay?"

The dragon sighed. "Oh, sure, make me live on bread and water. Keep me a prisoner in your room. I'll soon waste away to nothing, then you won't need to feed me at all." She sniffed, and inhaled deeply. "What's that *delightful* smell?"

Chrissie sniffed. "You mean the coffee?"

"Coffee?" The dragon looked happy. "That's what I'd like."

Chrissie looked at her dubiously. "I'd hate to think of you on a caffeine high."

"Please, please, please, please, please . . ."

"Oh, stop begging," Chrissie said. "Okay, I'll get you a cup. But only one." She took her empty oatmeal dish downstairs. Thankfully, Mom was getting her briefcase and papers ready for the office. She might wonder why Chrissie had suddenly taken to drinking coffee. Chrissie poured a cup and added some milk. Sugar? Probably—Kara had a bit of a sweet tooth. Then she took the cup upstairs. Kara virtually pounced on it, stuck her snout deep into the cup, and drank it down in almost one gulp.

"That's pretty good," she said, wiping her lips with her long tongue. "Can I have some more?"

"Maybe later," Chrissie said. "Too much caffeine can keep you awake. And you need to get some rest while I'm at school."

The dragon sighed. "So how long will you be gone?" she asked. "Ten minutes or so?"

"About six hours," Chrissie replied.

"Six hours?" Kara shook her head. "Oh, no. I'm not staying a prisoner in this room for six hours. I'll go mad!"

"You're already there," Chrissie growled. "Just stay put, stay hidden, and *behave* yourself, okay? We'll do something together when I come home—I promise."

"Huh!" the dragon complained. She glared at Chrissie. "That's it—abandon me. Leave me here to die of boredom. I don't care. Why should I expect to be treated well? I'm just a *dragon* after all." Muttering to herself, she slunk under the bed.

Chrissie rolled her eyes and went to brush her teeth. When she came out, she grabbed her backpack and headed for the door. "See you later," she called. There was no reply; obviously the dragon was still sulking at being left alone. Well, Chrissie would make it up later. She hoped Kara wouldn't cause any trouble during the day.

Chrissie had the strongest feeling that this would be unlikely. Having her own dragon would probably get her into trouble some-how. . . .

chapter
TWO

Chrissie clambered onto the school bus and sat down next to Jessica Bowen, her best friend. The bus started up again, trundling on to the next pickup spot. "So," she asked Jessica, "anything interesting happen to you?"

"No, same old boring life." Jessica was a bit on the chubby side, with long brown hair she was always twiddling. "How about you?"

Chrissie thought, just for a second, of saying: *Well, I went to another universe, met myself as a boy, saved that world, adopted a dragon, and learned magic.* But the impulse didn't last long. Nobody would believe her, and she'd probably get locked up in a mental ward in a straitjacket. "Same old same old," she said.

"You feeling better?" Jessica asked.

"Huh? Oh, yeah, yeah, I'm better." Chrissie almost forgot she was supposed to have been sick yesterday.

"You two are the most boring people in the world," said a familiar voice from behind them. They turned to see Henry Plunkett peering over the seat back at them. He was sitting alone. Henry *always* sat alone. He pushed his glasses up on his nose. "Didn't you watch the space shuttle launch this morning?"

"No, Henry," Jessica said. "We're not all space geeks, like you, you know."

"Just what I'd expect of a couple of doofuses like you," Henry snapped back. "One of the most historical events of this century, and I'll bet you were both just stuffing your faces and dreaming about the latest pop star you like."

Actually I was arguing with a dragon, Chrissie thought, but she knew what would happen if she said that. She knew better than to encourage Henry, but she had to ask: "So what's so important about another boring space shuttle launch? They happen all the time."

"Not like this one," Henry said, eager to show off his knowledge. "This one is carrying the ELEMENT package."

"Yawn," Jessica said.

"What's that?" asked Chrissie. There was something nagging at the back of her mind, but she couldn't quite drag it up. Probably nothing important.

"Earth-Linked Electronic Microwave Elementary Net Test," Henry answered.

"Can't you speak English?" Jessica demanded.

"Basically, it's a chain of satellites that will circle the Earth and create a new World Wide Web. The Internet, you know. What you log onto when you use computers. Assuming you even know how to type." Henry glared at them. "It's the next generation in communications."

"Maybe you'll learn how to communicate better," Jessica teased him. "As in *get a life*."

Henry stared at her with scorn. "I *have* a life. I'm going to become the world's greatest computer technician. Bigger than Bill Gates. Richer than Microsoft. That's where the big bucks are these days, you idiots. I know all about ELEMENT, and you don't have a clue."

"Yes, well, I'm sure it's fascinating," Chrissie said. "But it doesn't affect us, does it?"

"It affects everyone," Henry informed her. "It will replace all computer links in the world. All TV, radio, and telephones. All navigation signals. Everything will be different when this is up and working in a couple of days."

"Will *you* be different?" asked Jessica. "Or will you still be super-geek?"

"There's no point in talking to you," Henry said crossly.

"No, there isn't," agreed Jessica. "So why do you bother?" Henry's face vanished as he sat back down. Jessica rolled her eyes.

"Loser," she muttered.

"He could be worse," Chrissie whispered. She sometimes felt a bit guilty teasing Henry. He was an idiot, but he couldn't help it.

"Yes, he could be twins," Jessica said and laughed. Then she changed the subject, and they talked about music all the way to school. Jessica had bought a new CD, and wanted Chrissie to come over after school to listen to it. Chrissie had to get her mom's permission, but liked the idea.

At school they hurried inside before the bell rang. Chrissie needed to dump some stuff in her locker and check on her homework. Jessica went with her. Chrissie opened her locker, then swung her backpack around and unzipped it inside the locker.

Kara stared guiltily up at her from inside.

Panicking, Chrissie zipped the pack shut again. "Er . . . I've got to go to the bathroom," she said—the only excuse she could think of. "I'll be back in a second. Wait here!" She rushed down the hall and into the bathroom. Luckily, it was empty. She opened her backpack again and glared at Kara. "What are you doing here?" she cried. "I told you to stay at home!"

"I got bored," the dragon answered. "Besides, we're partners, so I have to be around in case you need me."

"I don't *need* you at school!" Chrissie exclaimed. "We don't do magic here!"

"You should," Kara said. "It would probably make the place more interesting." She grinned. "We could turn that Henry into a toad. . . ."

"Don't change the subject," Chrissie snapped. "Now what am I going to do? I can't take you home, and you can't stay. You're no good at following orders."

The door to the bathroom opened, and Miss Green looked in. Her eyes narrowed as she saw Kara. The dragon tried to duck down into the backpack again out of sight, but she wasn't fast enough. Miss Green had eyes that could spot a note being passed in class even with her back turned. There was no way she could miss seeing the dragon.

"Chrissie Scott!" she said severely. "You *know* that you're not allowed to bring pets to school!"

"I am not—" Kara started to say before Chrissie clamped her fingers over the dragon's snout.

"Bringing her to school," Chrissie continued, trying to make it sound as if she'd been the one speaking all along. "She sneaked into my pack this morning, and I only just found her."

"Well, you can just find your way to the principal's office, young lady," Miss Green said, sniffing in disapproval. "And see if he believes your story any more than I do."

Chrissie winced. That was all she needed—detention. . . . But there was nothing else for it. "Yes, Miss Green," she said sadly. Then she glared at the dragon. Some start to the day! Kara did have the grace to look ashamed, at least, but that didn't help now. Miss Green held the door open so Chrissie could walk out and go down the corridor.

Jessica ran to join her. "What happened?"

"I've got to go to see the principal," she replied.

"Wow, what did you do? Trash the toilet?"

Well, there was nothing else for it but to own up. Chrissie opened her backpack. Kara's face peeked out. The rest of the dragon's body was hidden among the books. Jessica's eyes went wide. "Hey, cute lizard! When did you get it?"

"Her," Chrissie said. "Her name's Kara. I got her yesterday. She was *supposed* to stay home while I was at school, but she sneaked into my pack instead."

Jessica nodded. "I can see why Greenie freaked out. And it's not even your fault, is it?"

"That's not how she sees it. Look, Jess, you'd better get along to class. I'll be there as soon as I find out my punishment."

Jessica nodded and hurried off. Chrissie entered the office and gave her name to the secretary. Then she sat down to await her doom. How could things get worse?

There was a hiccup from inside her bag, and a "pardon me" followed by the distinct smell of burning. Yelping, Chrissie pulled open her bag. Kara was beating out flames with her paws. She had set Chrissie's homework on fire! Chrissie batted out the small flames and looked at the charred top page in shock.

The secretary glared down at her. "What do you think you're doing, young lady?" she demanded. "Do you have *cigarettes* in there?"

Chrissie groaned. She was doomed. . . .

chapter
THREE

Chrissie's mood was really black when she headed back to class. The principal hadn't found cigarettes, of course, but neither had he found her explanation very convincing. He had confiscated Kara until the end of the day and was going to put her in one of the science labs. That scared Chrissie for two reasons: First, could the dragon be trusted to keep her mouth shut until the end of the day? And, second, what if one of the teachers got curious about what sort of a "lizard" she was and tried to find out? If they discovered they had an unknown species in their aquarium tank, what would they do then? At least Kara was keeping her wings tightly folded, so at a quick glance she *looked* very lizardlike.

And, on top of that, Chrissie had two hours of detention. A few days ago she would never have thought that detention would ever be the least of her problems.

Naturally, her homework had been ruined, which would cause *more* trouble. Who would have thought that being able to do magic could create such a mess?

Maybe she could use magic to get out of all of this. It was tempting, but the problem was that she was still very new at it, and didn't really know that much. She could produce fire, or make images appear in mirrors, and minor stuff like that, but she needed to study more to be able to do anything really good, like fly. Or get herself out of detention.

Time dragged. At the end of the first period, Jessica wanted to know what had happened, of course. And, naturally, everybody in class knew that Chrissie had brought a lizard to school and been punished for it, so there were a lot of cruel comments about that. Still, they were better than the ones from the animal lovers, who all wanted to go immediately to the science lab and pet Kara.

The only person who didn't seem interested in what she had done was Henry. He was too fascinated with his satellites to pay attention to what was happening in the real world. Since they had computers next, it didn't take Henry long to convince the teacher, Mr. Jensen, to check out the NASA Web site for information on how the space shuttle mission was going. So they all had to follow along and do the same thing.

Boring. What difference did the satellites make to anybody but computer nerds like Henry?

Once she had logged on, Chrissie just skimmed the information. The shuttle was in orbit, and getting ready to start putting out the ELEMENT satellites. Once again, Chrissie had a feeling that there was something she should know about this, but she couldn't remember what. She scrolled down the page, her eyes flicking about, not really reading the lines.

All at once she stopped and backed up. Had she seen what she thought . . . ? Yes, she had.

". . . the product of the computer genius Larry Lee and his team in Dallas . . ."

Larry Lee? That was an awful lot like the

name Lori Lee, the witch she had helped to defeat on the other world.

Then it all finally clicked. Now she knew what it was she'd forgotten! Everybody in this world had a double in the other, only of the opposite sex. So that meant that Lori Lee had to have a double in *this* world, a man. And since *she* had been scheming to take over *that* world . . .

"Oh, no," she muttered. Quickly Chrissie started to read the page again, this time paying careful attention to the article. It seemed that Larry Lee and his company had developed the ELEMENT satellites, and that they were going to change the whole communications industry. As Henry had explained earlier, ELEMENT was going to make computers, telephones, radios, televisions, and so on, all come under a single control. They'd be faster, better, more efficient.

And, Chrissie suspected, under Larry Lee's power. If he was anything like Lori Lee, he wasn't doing this out of the goodness of his heart. She searched for more information on Larry Lee and found that his company had its own Web site. When she checked that out, she knew her suspicions were correct.

Lori Lee had been in her late twenties, with pure white hair and pale skin. She always dressed in white, and the only color on her was her black eyes. Larry Lee was the male version of that—neatly trimmed white hair, a white suit and tie, and the same jet-black eyes.

Now what was she going to do? Obviously, the man was up to something with these satellites. Lori Lee had tried to rule her world by getting control of the Elementals that governed magic there. Larry Lee was using ELEMENT to do what? Rule the world, Chrissie was ready to bet.

But who would believe her if she tried to tell anyone? She was just a kid. Her teachers would never accept what she said, especially not after she had already been given detention. And if she tried to report Larry Lee to the police or some other group, she'd have even less luck. So what was she to do? She couldn't handle this herself. She needed help.

Which meant getting Kara back. With Kara's help, she should be able to do some magic. Not much, but enough maybe.

She stuck up her hand quickly. "Please,"

she said to Mr. Jensen, "I need to go to the bathroom."

"Oh, very well," he said crossly. "But don't take too long. I don't want you missing anything."

I won't miss anything useful, she thought as she hurried out and down to the science lab.

There was a class in there.

Chrissie winced. She peeked through the glass window in the door and spotted Kara in one of the tanks. The dragon looked as if she'd gone to sleep, so she wasn't causing any problems at least. But what was Chrissie to do? She couldn't just walk in and pick up Kara; the teacher was bound to object, and Chrissie would be sent off to the principal again. Chrissie bit her lip, wishing she could think of something brilliant, but her mind stayed obstinately empty.

"In trouble again, are you?" said a voice from down near the floor. Chrissie jumped and peered down. Her eyes widened in shock.

"Bellwether!" she exclaimed.

The large black cat nodded politely. "The same," he agreed and sat down to start licking his paws.

Bellwether was a magical cat from the other world. He had begun by being on Lori Lee's side, but then had switched sides to help Chrissie and Chris defeat the witch. The problem was, Chrissie didn't know if she could trust the cat, or whether he was just up to some devious plan of his own. The last time she had seen him, he had been on the other world. "However did you get here?" she asked.

"All cats can walk between the worlds," Bellwether replied. "We don't need *human* magic for that. People have always known we could do magic of our own. I seem to recall some story you humans tell about Puss in Boots. One of my own ancestors, in fact. A cheat, liar, and scoundrel." Bellwether smiled, which would certainly have terrified any mouse. "I'm very proud of him. But enough about me. What about you? You look like you could use some help."

Chrissie had no choice but to trust him for the moment, since there was nobody else to help her. So she explained what she had discovered, and what she suspected.

"It sounds perfectly reasonable to me," Bellwether agreed. "I was right, you do need help. First things first; we'd better get your dragon back to you."

"How can we do that?" Chrissie asked. "There's a class in there."

"For the moment," the cat agreed lazily. Then he sprang up into the air, and his paw darted out. For a moment what he was doing made no sense.

Until Chrissie saw the fire alarm box. . . .

Bellwether's paw slashed at the fire alarm, and immediately the hallway was filled with the braying sound.

Oh, no!

chapter
FOUR

Chrissie couldn't believe what Bell-wether had just done. Was the cat really trying to help her, or was he just trying to get her into trouble? "What have you done?" she asked, appalled. "I'm going to be in so much trouble if they find me here!"

"Then they'd better not find you here, had they?" Bellwether asked, unconcerned. He sat down and started cleaning his paws. "It doesn't matter about me, of course—everybody knows it couldn't be *me* who sounded the alarm. . . ."

Trying not to panic, Chrissie thought fast. She had about ten seconds before everyone would pour out of the classrooms—not long enough for her to sprint and hide in the bathroom. And if she was spotted running, everyone would be certain she had sounded the alarm.

Maybe she could start a real fire? She had the power to do that, she knew. But she also knew that that would be a foolish and dangerous act. The fire could easily get out of hand. But she couldn't be found here. . . .

Then the answer came to her. Kara was close enough for Chrissie to reach out to mentally feel the power the little dragon had. *"To-bira-re!"* she said in the magical language. She just hoped she'd got it right. She *thought* that it meant "Don't be seen," or in other words become invisible. But the expression *might* mean "Don't see anything," in which case Chrissie might make herself blind. Magic wasn't as easy as it seemed. . . .

Then the doors opened to the classrooms, and the pupils began filing out in neat lines, nobody running or yelling. In fact, most were trying hard not to laugh. They were all sure that it was just a drill or a prank, but they were going through the fire drill properly. Chrissie gulped and her stomach turned over—was she going to be spotted?

But nobody said anything to her, or even looked in her direction. She'd gotten the spell right! She *was* invisible! She wanted to laugh with relief, but she was only invisible, not inaudible. If she made any sound, somebody would hear her, and *that* would certainly cause problems. So she waited till the corridor was clear before dashing into the science lab.

"There you are," Kara grumbled. "I was getting very bored in here. I was just about ready to scream to be let out. It was cruel of you to abandon me." Kara was linked to her magically, so she obviously didn't need to *see* Chrissie to know where she was.

"It wasn't my idea," Chrissie snapped. "I *told* you to stay at home. How long will this invisibility spell last?"

Kara sniffed. "Not very long. Five minutes, maybe, from the time you cast it. It would have been stronger if you were closer to me."

"I was as close as I could get," Chrissie answered. She hauled Kara out of the aquarium tank, and the little dragon scuttled up to wrap herself around Chrissie's neck. Now what? She didn't have the time left on her spell to get out of school and off the grounds before becoming visible again. As soon as the teachers took roll call, they'd know she was missing and come looking for her. This whole thing was getting *way* too complicated, and she couldn't think fast enough to figure a way out of it. She badly needed the help of somebody better at magic than she was. But the constant whining of the fire alarm was making it hard for her to concentrate.

If only Bellwether hadn't set the alarm off! That cat was more of a nuisance working for her than he was working for the enemy! That is, if he had really switched sides. Maybe he was just trying to get her into trouble and keep her out of the way. . . .

The only thing she could think of was to hide. Supposedly she had been going to the bathroom, hadn't she? If Mr. Jensen had anyone look for her, that's the first place he'd check. Still invisible, she sprinted for the bathroom and dived inside. She jumped into one of the stalls and then, finally, had a bright idea. She needed an excuse not to be outside with the others. The stall had a door that went all the way to the floor. Maybe if the door was stuck . . . ?

At that moment she could hear somebody

coming down the corridor. Banging on the inside of the door, she yelled, "Help! Help! The door's stuck!" Kara got the idea, and used a tiny bit of magic to make the door expand a bit, so it was too tight to open easily. "You'd better hide," Chrissie whispered to her. "Unless you want to go back into that tank."

"No, thanks." Kara slid up the wall and knocked one of the ceiling tiles aside, slipping into the open space. "I'll wait up here for you. I'm kind of sleepy now."

Chrissie wondered if she was still invisible. If the stall door opened before she reappeared, she would have a lot of explaining to do.

The door to the bathroom opened and Miss Green called out: "Chrissie Scott? Is that you?"

"Yes," Chrissie answered, trying to sound relieved instead of scared. "I'm stuck in here. The door won't open."

"What nonsense is this?" Miss Green strode to the door and rattled it. It didn't budge. "Oh, it *is* stuck."

"I heard the alarm," Chrissie said truthfully. "But I couldn't get out."

"So I see. Wait a minute." Miss Green went

to the bathroom door and called for Mr. Jensen. With the two of them pulling on it, the stall door finally flew open. Both teachers stood outside, looking rather worried as well as annoyed. "Are you all right?" Miss Green asked.

"I am now," Chrissie said, and she wasn't lying. It looked as if she was out of trouble for now. Her invisibility spell had worn off just in time.

"To be honest, we thought that you must have set the fire alarm off," Mr. Jensen told her. "But if you were stuck in here . . ." He was suspicious, but he couldn't imagine how she could have jammed the door like that. Luckily he didn't believe in magic!

"Honestly," Chrissie swore, "I didn't touch the alarm. I was shocked when I heard it."

"Yes, well, you'd better go outside with the others," Mr. Jensen said. "The school has to be checked by the fire department before anyone is allowed back inside."

Chrissie nodded and hurried off through the nearest door with Miss Green. She had managed to rescue Kara, at least, so the dragon wouldn't cause a problem—until somebody noticed that she was missing, of course. It seemed as if magic wasn't the answer to every problem.

Chrissie rejoined her class on the sidewalk outside of school. The fire engines were just starting to arrive, ready to check for the non-existent fire. Chrissie bit at her lip. This was all Bellwether's fault! The cat was probably laughing to himself right now, enjoying the chaos he had caused.

Then she spotted him, being held very tightly by one of the third-graders. Bellwether appeared very uncomfortable but knew better than to speak or to claw his way free. He was having to suffer being squeezed very affectionately by his "rescuer."

That served the cat right! Chrissie couldn't help grinning at the sight. It was a small payback for the misdeeds of the cat, but it was somehow quite appropriate. She was glad Bellwether was suffering a little.

chapter
FIVE

It was half an hour before everyone was allowed back into the school. The principal was annoyed at the false alarm, and determined to discover who the prankster was. Chrissie was safe from suspicion because nobody could figure out how she could have been locked in the bathroom if she had set the alarm off. But she knew that she was being watched closely by the teachers, which wouldn't make her task any easier.

She was certain that Larry Lee had to be as evil as his alter ego Lori Lee on the magical world. It had taken her, Chris, and Chris's sister, Sam, to stop Lori Lee. Chrissie knew that she needed help, and the only person who would believe her totally was Chris.

That meant summoning him from his world. She couldn't do that while school was in session, but how long would it be before Larry Lee's plan—whatever it was—went too far to be stopped?

Much as she hated the thought, she needed information, and the only person she knew who had it was Henry Plunkett. He was a boring idiot, but he really knew about this ELEMENT stuff. She was going to have to talk to him. She'd almost rather be at the dentist without anesthetic. And, of course, she couldn't tell him why she wanted to know about Larry Lee all of a sudden.

Why was life so complicated?

As soon as she finished eating her lunch, Chrissie steeled herself and went to talk to Henry. He blinked a lot and stared at her through his glasses in surprise. "I didn't think you cared about computers," he said.

Chrissie shrugged. "Well, you said it was so important, so I figured I should know *something* about it all. I don't want to be stupid, do I?"

"Too late," Henry said, and she wanted to punch him for that. Then he shrugged.

"Okay, I guess I can explain it if you really want to know."

"You said that this is going on right now," Chrissie reminded him. "Just what, exactly, is happening?"

"Well, the latest space shuttle is taking up the final four satellites," Henry answered. "There's a whole bunch of them up there already, circling Earth. They're just waiting for the final satellites to be launched and get into position. These four satellites will control the others, and together they can broadcast signals to the whole of Earth. Every single electronic device that normally uses telephone lines can be brought under the system. Telephones, computers, emergency signals, police, fire, ambulances—television and radio. Everything that makes civilization work."

Chrissie began to get the picture and realized just what Larry Lee was up to. These days *everything* was controlled by computers. News was spread by TV and radio. People talked to one another over the telephone. If Larry Lee could control ELEMENT, then he would control all of the machinery, all of the news, and all communication. Without his permission, people would be cut off from everything.

It was exactly the same sort of thing that Lori Lee had tried to do on her magical world—take over the world by controlling the way things ran. And here was Larry Lee on her world aiming to do the same thing. According to Henry's research, Larry Lee was this really nice, dedicated man who had built dozens of satellites for NASA, so the government obviously trusted him. Chrissie realized that his niceness had to be an act, just as it had been with Lori Lee. But she knew nobody in authority would ever believe her. She had to stop him herself—but how? And how long did she have?

"When will these satellite thingies be ready to use?" she asked Henry.

"In about six or seven hours, I should think," Henry replied. "They've already launched the four satellites into space. Now NASA is just positioning them and then they'll test them. Once everybody is sure they're in working order, they'll start the ELEMENT program running."

That would be the end of the free world, Chrissie realized. *Six or seven hours . . .* there was no time to waste. She knew she was going to get into trouble for this, but she was going to have to cut school and suffer the consequences later. She *had* to get to Chris now, and that meant collecting Kara and doing magic.

"Thanks, Henry," she said. She was quite surprised to discover he wasn't as bad as she had always thought. He'd been nice and helpful and actually explained things so she could understand them. He seemed to be enjoying the attention she was paying him. Normally everybody just ignored him, so this was clearly a new experience for Henry. She just hoped that he wasn't getting the wrong idea from all of this. "I've got to run. Got to go to the bathroom."

"Maybe you should see a doctor," Henry suggested. "You seem to be going an awful lot today."

Chrissie sighed and hurried off. There was another girl in the bathroom, so Chrissie stood there until the girl left and she was alone. "Kara!" she called. There was no answer. Had the dragon become bored and gone exploring or something? No, Chrissie discovered, as she reached out mentally. She could feel Kara there, still in the ceiling. "Kara!" she called louder.

"Leave me alone," the dragon grumbled. "I'd just fallen asleep."

"This isn't the time for sleeping," Chrissie said. "This is the time for action."

"Oh, right, so you just have to wake me up and make me work. I'm a growing dragon; I need my rest."

"Rest later," Chrissie snapped. "Come on down."

"Oh, all right." There was a noise in the ceiling tiles, and then Kara dropped down into Chrissie's open arms. "But you owe me for this."

At that moment the door to the bathroom opened and Jessica walked in. "Chrissie, are you okay? I saw you talking . . ." Her voice trailed off as she saw Kara slip up Chrissie's arm, and wrap herself around Chrissie's neck. "Chrissie! You're going to get into trouble! You know what Miss Green will do if she catches you!"

"Bother Miss Green," Kara snapped. "And bother you, too."

Chrissie groaned as Jessica's eyes opened wide in shock. "That *lizard* spoke!"

"I'm not a lizard, I'm a dra—"

Chrissie clamped her hand around Kara's snout. "Will you please shut up!" she exclaimed. "You've caused enough trouble as it is." She looked at her friend. "Jessica, I promise I'll explain all of this later, but right now I don't have the time."

"What *is* that thing?" Jessica asked, ignoring Chrissie. "How come it can talk? Is it like a parrot?"

"A *parrot?*" Kara yelled, struggling free of Chrissie's grip. "I've never been so insulted in my life! I ought to bite you for that!" She showed her sharp teeth. "Don't you know a dragon when you see one?" Then she spread her tiny wings. Jessica's eyes grew huge.

Chrissie groaned. "Will you *shut up!*" she growled. "You're only making things worse!"

"A *dragon?*" Jessica asked, astonished. She clearly believed Kara, and why shouldn't she? "That is just so cool, Chrissie. Can I pet her?"

"I am *not* a pet," Kara said huffily. "I'm a magician. But you can scratch my chin if you like."

"No!" Chrissie said before Jessica could move. "This isn't the time for scratching, or explaining, or anything. I've only got about six hours to save the world, and I'm not wasting time with either of you." She stared hard at her friend. "And if you don't leave this room right now, I'm not going to be responsible for your sanity."

"I'm not going anywhere," Jessica promised, "until I know what's going on."

Chrissie was too annoyed and tense to argue. "Suit yourself," she agreed. Then she tapped Kara on the head. "Right, concentrate . . ." She looked into the mirror on the wall. *"To-nama!"* she ordered it. *Be fluid!* It was how Chris had cast the spell to transfer her to his world. She just hoped it worked the reverse way.

The mirror abruptly became cloudy, then cleared again, and showed the scene as before. Except this time, she wasn't looking at her own reflection. She was looking at a boy who looked a lot like her—blond hair, T-shirt, jeans, and sneakers. It was her double on the magical world, Chris.

"Chrissie!" Chris exclaimed. "What's wrong? Why are you . . . ?" His voice trailed off as he saw Jessica, her eyes bulging in shock behind his twin. "Who's that?"

"There's no time to explain," Chrissie told

him. "You have to come through to my world, right now. I really need your help!"

Chris hesitated just a second. He'd get into trouble for missing classes, too, she knew. But he knew she wouldn't do this without a very good reason. "Right," he agreed, and held out his hands. Jessica screeched in shock as the two hands came *through* the mirror. Chrissie grabbed them and pulled him through. Jessica was yelping like a puppy and backed up into the far wall.

"What's happening?" she asked, shaking.

"Magic," said another voice. Chris had a firedrake, Redfire, as his own partner. This was another lizardlike creature, like a minor dragon, and he was wrapped about Chris's neck. He opened an eye to speak, then went back to sleep.

"I don't believe it," Jessica said weakly. She looked pale and shocked.

"It's your own fault," Chrissie said without sympathy. "I told you not to stay. You should have listened to me."

"And missed all of this?" Jessica asked. She shook her head. "This is *way* too cool!"

At that moment the door opened again, and Miss Green stepped inside. Behind her in the corridor, Chrissie saw Henry, looking worried. He must have gone to fetch a teacher, thinking there was something wrong with Chrissie.

Well, there certainly was now!

"Chrissie Scott!" Miss Green snapped, raging. "Jessica Bowen! What are you doing in the girls' bathroom with a *boy?*"

Chrissie winced. The only thing worse than what it looked like was if somebody tried to tell the teacher the truth. Which she knew Jessica would blurt out in just a couple of seconds. . . .

chapter
SIX

"I suppose it's up to me to save the day," Redfire said gloomily. "It's always work for me."

Miss Green stared at the firedrake in shock. "What *is* that horrible thing?" she demanded. "Is this a plague of lizards today?"

"This will be a pleasure," Redfire announced. His eyes burned as he stared back at the teacher. "Listen to me. There is nothing wrong here. Everything is just fine. You will go back to your duties and remember only that everything is okay."

Miss Green blinked and shook herself. "Of course everything is okay," she said and sniffed. "It always is when I'm around." She turned and marched out of the bathroom.

Jessica was impressed. "Wow! Could you do that to make her forget to give us home-work?" she asked Redfire.

"We're not here to dodge work," Chris said before Redfire could agree. "What's wrong, Chrissie?"

Chrissie sighed. Redfire's ability to influ-ence people's minds had come in handy again, but it didn't get them out of all of their trouble. "There's somebody you have to talk to," she told her twin. She led them all out of the bathroom. Henry was still in the corridor, looking worried and guilty.

"You're not upset with me, are you?" he asked hastily. "I only told Miss Green because I thought you were sick."

"No," Chrissie assured him. "Actually, I was quite touched that you cared enough. But right now you've got some explaining to do. Tell my . . . cousin here all about ELEMENT."

That took some doing. Chris was from a world where there was no such thing as sci-ence, so he didn't have the vaguest idea what a computer or a space shuttle or a satellite might be. Henry found it hysterically funny that any kid, even a friend of Chrissie's, could be so dumb. The only way to stop him laughing and get him talking again was to tell him the truth. He and Jessica listened to Chrissie's story about Larry Lee with wide eyes. The only reason neither of them laughed was the presence of the dragons.

Chrissie couldn't see any point in trying to keep her secret from the two of them. When lunch ended, she told Jessica and Henry to remain where they were. "We're going to have to skip classes," she said. "We may get into trouble, but we've got to stop Larry Lee. I think saving the world is a bit more important than getting detention, don't you?"

Jessica had to think about that for a minute. Then she brightened. "We could always get Redfire to explain it to people," she suggested. Chrissie had to admit that this was a good idea.

They went to the computer lab, which was fortunately free this period. Chris was astonished at his first computer and kept laughing and trying to understand it. "Electricity!" he exclaimed. "It's almost like magic!"

Henry booted up the computer and used it to show Chris pictures from the space shutle. Eventually Chris got the idea. "This is really wild," he said enthusiastically. "I could get to like this world."

"Yes, well, first we've got to save it," Chrissie pointed out. "As soon as those satellites are operational, Larry Lee will control *everything* on this planet. And if he's like his alter ego, he's going to use that power to seize control of everything. He could shut down hospitals, factories—even whole cities. And nobody will ever believe he'd do anything like that because in the past he's always been very careful to act like the good guy. If it wasn't that I knew what Lori Lee was like, even I wouldn't have suspected him."

"That sounds all too likely," Chris agreed. "But how can we stop him? This is your world, not mine."

"I don't know," Chrissie answered. "I was sort of hoping that Henry would have an idea."

"Henry Plunkett?" Chris asked. "I know your other self in my world—Hannah. She's a bit of a *kleep*, I'm afraid. Totally into wacky spells."

"I don't know what a *kleep* is," Henry

said with a sigh, "but I have a suspicion."
He pushed his glasses back up his nose.
"It's the price you pay for being too interested in things." Chrissie was starting to
realize that she'd been way too harsh with
Henry, simply because he liked to do things
she didn't. And here she was now relying
on him. It would serve her right if he
refused. "Okay," Henry said. "There's only
one way to stop Larry Lee that I can think
of. We have to stop the satellites from going
operational."

"How can we do that?" Chrissie asked.

"I don't know," Henry answered. "They're
powering up now. Maybe if we could stop
them at NASA, get them to turn the power
off." He shook his head. "They'd never
believe us, at least not in time."

"Maybe we could stop Larry Lee from using
the satellites?" suggested Jessica.

Chrissie thought hard. "I don't think we
could do that, either," she said. "That would
involve more science than even Henry
knows. Maybe we could just destroy the
satellites? It's always easier to break something than fix it."

Henry stared at her. "Those satellites cost

millions of dollars! They'd stop your allowance for the rest of your life. And, anyway, how could we destroy them? They're in *space*, and we're here on Earth."

Chrissie looked at Chris. "Could we use magic to go into space?" she asked.

"I don't know," he confessed. "I've heard that it's possible. Nelly Armstrong managed to get to the Moon once. But it takes a lot of specialized knowledge, I should think. I don't have a clue how to do it."

Neither did Chrissie, but she couldn't afford to let that stop her. "What would we need to know?" she asked Henry.

"We'd need to know their exact position," he answered slowly. "Space is really big, and they're really small. You'd have to be very accurate. But how could you blow them up?"

"We don't need to blow them up," Chrissie said. "We just need to make sure they don't work properly. That would be enough. Now, where would the information about their exact positions be? Could you find it online?"

Henry gave her a where's-your-brains look. "They don't put that sort of information on the net," he told her. "It will only be inside NASA's computers, or maybe Larry Lee has it."

"Larry Lee," Chrissie and Chris said together. "We'll have to get it from him."

"Uh, guys," Henry pointed out. "He's in Dallas, Texas, not the next street."

Chris shrugged. "So we go to Dallas, Texas," he said. "No big deal."

"It's thousands of miles away, and we don't have the airfare," Henry said. "Or the time."

"What's *airfare?*" Chris asked.

"We'll use a magical way to get there *really* fast," Chrissie said. "How about some sort of transport spell?"

"I don't know any," Chris confessed. "But I do know a magic carpet spell."

"Magic carpet?" Jessica squealed. "Oh, that is *so* neat!"

"It's just for him and me," Chrissie warned her friend.

"Oh, right," Henry said, sniffing. "And what will you do about getting the information you need without me along?"

"And if he goes, I go," Jessica insisted. "I always wanted to do an Aladdin!"

Chris shrugged. "As long as the carpet's big

enough, there shouldn't be a problem," he said.

No problem! Chrissie groaned to herself. It looked as if they had nothing *but* problems. "Oh, all right," she agreed, knowing she couldn't win. "But I just know I'm going to regret this. . . ."

chapter
SEVEN

Chris decided that the carpet in the computer room would be fine for their trip. "We'd better take it outside, though," he said. "Once it gets going, the carpet should really move." He cast what he called a don't-look-at-me spell. Nobody paid any attention while the four of them dragged the carpet out of the school and into the parking lot.

Jessica eyed it with obvious worry. "Won't we fall off it?" She shuddered at the thought of dropping from a carpet hundreds of feet in the air.

"Hey, this is elementary magic," Chris protested. "Trust me, I could do this in my sleep. Hey, Redfire, wake up."

The little firedrake yawned. "I suppose this means work again? Doesn't this planet have laws against slavery?"

"Only for human beings," Chrissie told him, grinning. Redfire was always complaining about being overworked, though he spent most of his life asleep.

"That figures," the firedrake replied, sniffing. "Prejudice!"

"Stop complaining, and help me get this right," Chris said. "Okay, everybody on the carpet." Chrissie felt a bit foolish sitting on the computer room carpet in the parking lot of her school. So, too, from the look of things, did Jessica and Henry. But they did as they were told. Kara snuggled happily around Chrissie's neck, apparently fast asleep and unbothered by what was happening.

Chris concentrated, sitting at the front of the carpet. *"To-chapa!" Be attached!* Chrissie felt some force like an invisible hand holding her in place. Jessica gave a squeal as she obviously felt the same effect. *"Maktar, to-fiva!" Carpet, fly!*

The carpet gave a shudder, then rippled underneath them. Jessica squealed again. Chrissie and the others rose from the ground, apparently held up by only the threads of a carpet. It wavered and shivered but seemed firm enough.

Then it shot into the sky so fast she almost screamed. Jessica and Henry did scream, which annoyed the dragon. Kara put claws over her ears. The ground dropped away really fast as the carpet zipped into the air. It must have risen a couple of thousand feet before finally leveling off. Chrissie was quite breathless.

The view was staggering. She'd been on a plane once, when the family had gone to Disney World, but that was nothing like this! Then she'd been in an air-conditioned cabin, on a comfy seat, with flight attendants bringing them drinks and food. On the carpet they weren't inside anything. All around them was space. Chrissie didn't even have to lean over the edge of the carpet to see the ground way below them. At least it wasn't cold.

"I *really* hope you know what you're doing," Chrissie said to her twin.

He grinned back at her. "This isn't a spell you can mess up," he told her. "They wouldn't allow you to do it if it was dangerous, would they?"

"I guess not," Chrissie admitted. "But it's still kind of scary." And exciting, of course. She felt the air flowing past her and saw the land scurrying along underneath them. She wondered if anyone was looking up, and if so, what they would think they were seeing.

Henry was quite pale, but seemed to be determined not to show how frightened he was. Jessica had settled down and seemed to be enjoying herself, trying to pick out landmarks below them.

Then Chris screamed.

Chrissie, terrified that something had gone wrong, looked where he was staring in horror. "What is that monster?" he howled.

Chrissie laughed. "It's an airplane," she told him. It was a jet, obviously only just taken off from a local airport, because it was still rising. It was only about five hundred feet away, and Chrissie wondered if it was too close. But the carpet didn't seem bothered by it and kept moving steadily on as the plane rose upward toward the clouds.

"Hey, they've seen us!" Jessica said, and started waving madly at the plane.

"What *is* it?" Chris asked again, still shaking.

"Well, we don't have dragons," Chrissie explained. "Or flying carpets. So when we want to go long distances, we use those things. They're called aircraft, and they fly using jet engines. It's a science thing."

"It looks way too heavy to fly without a good levitation spell," Chris muttered. But he did seem to be calming down. Chrissie couldn't blame him, really. Nothing like a plane existed on his world. It had to be as scary to him as seeing her first dragon had been to her.

The pilot had definitely spotted the carpet by now. There were two other men leaning over to stare out his window, also. Chrissie, feeling a bit light-headed, blew them a kiss. The three men all rubbed their eyes, obviously not believing what they were seeing.

"You think they'll report us?" Jessica asked.

"Not if they want to keep their jobs," Henry said firmly. "A flying saucer is one thing, but a flying carpet is quite another!"

Some of the passengers had spotted the carpet, too, and a couple of them waved back rather nervously. But the carpet was moving far faster than the jet, and they pulled out of sight quickly. Chrissie couldn't help wondering what the passengers and crew made of their odd sighting!

They didn't come as close to any other planes on their flight, thankfully, though they did spot plenty in the distance. Chris calmed down a bit when he understood that they weren't monsters, and enjoyed discussing flying with Henry—who, of course, knew everything there was to know on the subject.

Chrissie was surprised that the carpet didn't need steering. "It's all done by willpower," Chris explained. "I'm guiding it mentally."

Redfire opened one eye. "Who is?" he asked pointedly.

"Okay, we're doing it together," Chris admitted. "But, whatever, it will go where we want it to, no problem."

"I hope you're right," Chrissie muttered. It wasn't that she didn't trust Chris, it was just that using magic was way too new to her to believe in it wholeheartedly. What if the spell failed for some reason? They would fall back to Earth and die, and she found she just couldn't ignore this.

Kara stirred, and poked her face into

Chrissie's. "Are you always this gloomy?" she asked. "Only seeing the dark side of things?" Chrissie realized she should have known that the dragon would pick up on her thoughts.

"It's scary," she confessed.

"Right. And sitting in a big metal machine flying through the air isn't?" The dragon shrugged. "I definitely think this is the safer way to travel. Stop worrying—if the spell was about to go wrong for any reason, I'd know and I'd tell you. I wouldn't want to have to break in a new partner."

That comforted Chrissie a bit, so she tried to stop worrying and concentrate on what they were doing. "What are we going to do when we get to Larry Lee's?" she asked. "I mean, we can't just march in and ask him if he's planning to rule the world and then call the cops on him."

"I guess we just wait till we get there and see what happens," Chris said.

"I'd feel happier if we had a bit of a plan," Chrissie answered.

Henry cleared his throat. "Whatever he's doing, the information will have to be in his computers. If I can check them, we might be able to find proof. Then we can take that to the police."

"There you are," Chris said cheerfully. "A plan."

"You call that a plan?" Chrissie asked him. "You don't think Larry Lee is going to let us look at his secret files, do you?"

"I'm very good with computers," Henry protested. "I'm sure I can find what we need."

"Besides, we can't whip up a better plan until we know what we're up against," Chris pointed out. "And we won't know what that is until we arrive at his headquarters. So just enjoy the view and the flight for now."

"Don't we get an in-flight movie?" Jessica asked cheekily. "Or at least a bag of pea-nuts?"

"Sorry, this is just a short flight," Chrissie answered pertly. She wasn't happy, but she knew Chris was right. They could spend for-ever coming up with plans, but unless they had specific information, all their planning might be worthless.

It took them less than an hour to reach Dallas. The city came up on them suddenly, and now the carpet slowed and began to descend.

"People are going to see us," Chrissie pointed out, worried.

"So what?" asked Henry. "They're hardly likely to call the police and report a flying carpet. Maybe the *National Enquirer* . . ."

They were heading for a large skyscraper in the business district, which was obviously the home of Larry Lee's company. Chris looked at the huge building in some shock. "Boy, you grow them big on this planet," he commented. "So which floor is Larry Lee going to be on?"

Chrissie grinned; there was only one possibility. "The penthouse," she said at exactly the same moment Henry did. Great minds thinking alike. Somebody with that big an ego would *have* to be on top of the world, looking down on everyone else.

"Right," Chris agreed, and mentally steered the carpet up to the top of the building. They passed by windows where they could see people working hard. Hard enough, thankfully, that none of them looked out to see four kids on a carpet flying past.

"That's his office," Chrissie said with certainty. Chris brought the carpet to a halt, and they looked inside. It was quite stark, with a simple, uncluttered desk and a few chairs.

"How do you know?" asked Chris, curiously.

"All of the others were small," she pointed out. "And they were packed. This one is big and empty. It's got to be his."

"Surprisingly logical for a human," Kara agreed.

"Okay." Chris was convinced. "Then let's go in and check it out."

"How do we do that?" asked Henry. "I'll bet there's a burglar alarm on it."

Chrissie stared at him, astonished. "This is on the eighty-something floor," she said. "Who'd expect burglars to get in?"

"From the roof," Henry answered. "Besides, Larry Lee is the sort of man who doesn't take chances."

Kara unwrapped herself and sniffed at the window. "There's some sort of a warning device," she agreed. "It's set off if you open the window."

"Then we'll go in without opening the window," Chris said simply. *"To-nama!" Be fluid!* Then he grinned at them all. "Come on." He stepped off the carpet and *through* the glass of the window. Since the window wasn't open, this didn't set off the alarm.

Gulping, and trying not to think about how far she'd fall if she misstepped, Chrissie followed him. It felt good when there was a nice, solid, unmoving carpet under her feet again. Henry and Jessica followed them in. Chris reached out and pulled in the carpet, which suddenly flopped back to being a normal carpet on the floor again.

"Now we look for clues," Chris said. But that was easier said than done. There wasn't a sign of anything in the office to search. There wasn't even a phone on the desk.

chapter

EIGHT

"How would a good burglar go about this?" Chrissie whispered.

"I don't know," Jessica replied. "Maybe there's a hidden safe?"

"Oh, right," Henry said sarcastically. "He'll have a big envelope in it marked *My Plan to Take Over the World.*" He shook his head. "He'll have any information we need on his computer."

"I don't even see a computer," Chrissie said. She looked at Chris. "Do you?"

"I'm not sure I know what a computer looks like," he said.

This wasn't going to be easy.

Henry walked across the white carpet to

the huge, empty desk and stared down at the glass top. "It's got to be here," he said. "Larry Lee isn't a man who wouldn't have everything where he needed it." He sat down in the chair and reached out to touch the top of the desk. Nothing happened.

"So much for that idea," Jessica said with a sniff.

"No," Chrissie said, grinning. "Don't forget that Larry Lee is six feet tall! He'd have longer arms than you."

"Of course," Henry agreed, slapping himself on the forehead. He bent down and looked across the glass. "Yes! I can see fingerprints!" Then he reached out a bit farther and tapped the top of the desk.

Immediately a screen set into the desk lit up. Everybody crowded around Henry and stared at it over his shoulders. A keyboard under the glass appeared as well, and Henry started tapping on it. Chrissie was amazed at how fast he could type. He somehow called up an inventory, though she didn't have a clue how he'd managed that. Then Access Denied appeared in the screen. Henry didn't seem to be put off, however, and he continued working. Chrissie didn't have a clue what he was doing, but whatever it was, it wasn't working. Chris got bored since he didn't understand any of this, and wandered off to check out the rest of the office. Jessica decided to look for a hidden safe anyway, even though there weren't any pictures on the walls. Chrissie stayed with Henry, certain that the answers would be in the computer.

Finally Henry sighed and shook his head. "He's got all the files too well guarded," he said. "I can't break any of the passwords. I don't know what to do now."

Kara opened an eye and scratched her neck with her back leg. "Secrets, eh? I'm good at secrets." She looked up at Chrissie. "Do you think you might be able to concentrate your mind just a little bit? It would be ever so helpful." Chrissie rolled her eyes; she hated being told off by a dragon, but she did as Kara said. The dragon concentrated hard and then stared intently at the computer.

It seemed to go haywire, lights flashing and numbers flickering over the screen.

"Did we set off an alarm?" Chrissie asked, scared that armed guards would burst through the door any second.

"No," Henry replied. "The system's just going crazy."

Kara sniffed. "Try it now," she suggested. "Computers! Easy stuff!" And she settled back to sleep.

Henry started typing again, and he laughed. "That dragon of yours is good," he said.

"*Very* good," Kara muttered.

"Very good," he agreed. "I'm into the files. It'll take me a little while to figure out what we need, though." He was entranced, working like crazy. Chrissie was glad he'd come along, since she didn't have a clue what he was doing. She went to join Chris.

"One thing I don't get," Chris told her. "Larry Lee's plan is almost working—so where is he? Shouldn't he be here, celebrating or something?"

"Maybe he's in his hidden control center somewhere," she suggested. "He's probably got a lot of things to do."

"Maybe." Chris had an ear to the door. "But I can't hear a sound outside in the corridor, and that's got to be odd. We saw plenty of people working as we arrived."

"Probably good soundproofing," Chrissie

said. "He's the boss, and he wouldn't want to listen to a lot of noise."

"Maybe," Chris agreed, but something was still bothering him.

"Got it!" Henry called. "Come and look at this, guys."

They hurried back to the desk. Jessica gave up tapping the walls for secret panels and joined them in looking at the screen again. Henry had a picture of the Earth up, showing the four satellites in orbit.

"Larry Lee has all the access codes to control the satellites," Henry explained. "Once they're turned on, he'll be able to take control of them and then he'll control the world's communications."

"Which is what we thought all along," Chrissie said. "Okay, but if he can take it over, can't NASA take it back?"

"That's what's so puzzling," Henry informed her. "If he was just beaming control from here, he could switch the passwords and lock everybody out. But then NASA could break his passwords and take control back again, just like you said. So I checked, and his control isn't coming from down here. It's coming from up there." He pointed to the ceiling.

"On the roof?" Jessica asked, confused.

"Higher," Henry told her. "Much higher."

"Space," Chrissie guessed, and he nodded. She frowned. "But how can he do that? Maybe one of the astronauts on the shuttle is secretly working for him?"

"That's one possibility," Henry agreed. "After all, once he takes control of ELE-MENT, the only way NASA could get it back is to launch another shuttle to go to alter the satellites. . . ."

"And the shuttle is computer controlled," Chrissie realized. "So he'd just make certain it never took off. Once he has control of the satellites, then *nothing* can switch them back."

"Right." Henry shook his head. "It's really well planned," he said admiringly. "Unless we stop him *before* he takes over the satellites, it'll be too late."

Chrissie thought about it. "Can you send this computer file to NASA?" she asked. "They wouldn't believe us if we called them and warned them because they trust him, but if they read Larry Lee's files, they'd believe those."

"Sure," Henry agreed. "I'll do it right away.

But the problem is that the people at NASA might not read this stuff immediately. And once they do, it might be *after* the satellites are locked."

Chrissie saw his point. "Well, send the stuff anyway," she decided. "We may get lucky."

"And if we don't?" asked Chris.

"Then we'll have to be creative," she replied. She didn't have a clue how they could do that, though. She hoped something would occur to her.

Henry looked up from his typing. "Okay, I sent the file," he said. "Now we just wait and hope?"

"No, we don't dare do that," Chrissie said. "We need to make sure Larry Lee is stopped. Can you use that computer to find out where he is?"

Henry shrugged. "It's worth a try." He started typing again and grinned. "Yes, all the employees in this building wear security badges. They're constantly being monitored, though they don't know it. Larry Lee doesn't trust anybody, and he isn't taking any chances that one of them is a spy. He's got it set up so that if anybody enters a secure area, alarms will go off here and in the security office." Then he frowned. "But I can't find Larry Lee anywhere in the building."

"Maybe he's not here," Jessica suggested.

"Where else would he be?" asked Henry.

"I don't know," Chrissie replied. "But if he really isn't here, we don't have a chance of finding him and stopping him in time. It can't be more than an hour or so till the satellites are all ready. We don't have time left to hunt for him."

chapter
NINE

Chrissie knew that she was the leader of this small group, and that it was up to her to come up with ideas. But she was completely out of them right now. If Larry Lee wasn't here, he could be almost anywhere. They didn't have much chance of finding him in the next hour if they didn't know where to look.

"Couldn't we just ask his secretary?" Jessia suggested.

Chrissie shrugged. "If we knew where she was, maybe. But she's probably with him."

Jessica, however, was stubbornly certain her idea was right, and was still thinking about a hidden safe. "What's in those areas that Larry Lee keeps people out of?" she asked Henry. "I'll bet that's where all his secret stuff is stored."

Henry shrugged. Since nobody had a better idea, he went ahead and checked. He called up a map of the building on the computer screen. It was in 3-D, and some areas were marked in red. He tried the first, and it pulled up a picture of a computer room. "Well, this one's the payroll area," he said. "I guess he doesn't want anybody giving himself a big bonus from Father Christmas."

"Father Christmas?" Chris laughed. "That's funny. On our world, it's a fat, jolly lady named Mary Christmas."

"Weird," Henry said. "But not useful." He pointed to a second area and pulled up another picture. "This one is where he parks his car. Ooh, nice color! I always wanted a red Porsche when I was old enough to drive. And this one . . ." He scowled. "This one has to be a mistake. It says it's a matter transmitter."

"A *what?*" asked Jessica.

"A matter transmitter," Henry repeated. "You know, like those transporters they use on *Star Trek*. They beam you from one place to another."

"Cool!" Jessica liked the sound of that.

"Yes, but impossible," Henry said. "They don't exist. They couldn't really work."

"Why not?" asked Chrissie.

"Well, let's just say that if one *did* exist, it would have to scan every single atom in a body at any given moment. Then it would have to turn all of those atoms into some sort of energy beam, and then re-create the same atoms at the end of the beam." Henry shook his head. "To do any of that takes time. No matter how fast a transmitter works, atoms move faster. They wouldn't be in the same place they started when the scanning was over. So you'd end up being a reconstituted mess if they could send you through a beam. And what sort of beam could carry all the information needed to re-create a living being?"

"So you're saying that it's impossible?" Chrissie repeated.

"Yes."

"Then why does Larry Lee think he's got one?" Chrissie had a feeling that this was the most important thing that they'd found. Maybe even more important than the satellites.

"I don't know," Henry confessed.

Chris shrugged. "We do this transporter thing all the time where I come from. It's pretty simple magic."

"Magic, maybe," Henry said stubbornly. "But it's not science. And on this world science rules."

"But *our* magic works," Chrissie said slowly. "So magic *could* work here, couldn't it?"

Henry gaped at them. "You two think he's using *magic?*"

Chris shrugged. "If science can't do it, and magic can . . . You know what the great detective Shirley Holmes always said: If you eliminate the impossible, whatever is left—however improbable—must be the truth."

"That's Sherlock Holmes," Chrissie muttered. "But it's still true. If a matter transmitter is scientifically impossible, maybe it's magically possible."

"There's only one way to find out," Henry said. "We'll have to take a look at it."

"How?" Jessica asked. "It's in a secure area."

"I can make us passes," Henry replied.

"I've got control of Larry Lee's computer, don't forget."

"That's no good," Chrissie pointed out. "The people here are bound to get suspicious of four kids with top security clearances, aren't they?"

"I guess so," Henry agreed, bothered he hadn't thought of that.

"Make the passes anyway," Chris said. "We'll need them to get through these machines of yours."

"Hey!" Jessica said brightly. "You said that this transporter thing is something you can do easily. Can't you just magic us inside that room?"

"Four of us?" Chris shook his head. "I'm not that good at magic. Even with Chrissie's help, we couldn't manage both of you as well. Besides, I don't know where the room is. I have to know where I'm going before I can get there. That's why I didn't transport us here and had to use the carpet instead. I could magic myself back to your school without any problem since I've already been there. But not to somewhere I've never been."

Chrissie frowned. "You did that on your own world when we were chasing Lori Lee."

"But I had her coordinates," Chris answered. "I just followed her spells. She was so much better at magic than I am, don't forget."

"Oh, right." Chrissie thought about it. "Okay, how about we turn all four of us invisible, and we walk there without being seen?"

"That could work," Chris agreed. "Invisibility is a lot easier than transport." He nudged Redfire. "How long would we be able to hold an invisibility spell?"

Redfire, grumbling, opened an eye. "Well, you and Chrissie are getting weaker at magic the longer you're away from the magic world. Even we won't be able to help you if your magic runs down. So, to turn four of you invisible? Fifteen minutes, tops."

"Would that be long enough?" Chrissie asked Henry. "How long would it take us to get to that room?"

"It's not that simple," Chris pointed out. "If people start seeing doors opening by themselves, they're going to realize something's up. And we'd have to hold hands, since we wouldn't be able to see one another, either. Somebody could walk into us—this is a crowded building. All of that means it's going to take us longer to get there than you'd think. Invisibility isn't the wonderful answer you might think."

"I'm open to better ideas," Chrissie said a bit more sharply than she intended. "We haven't got a lot of time, and I can't think of anything else to try."

Chris shrugged. "Neither can I," he confessed. "So I guess we go with your plan. Redfire, come on, help out here."

"Work, work, work," the firedrake complained. "That's all you ever want of me."

"Just do it."

Henry grinned and held up the four passes he'd created on the computer. "One each," he said, distributing them. "They'll get us anywhere, since I gave them the same clearance Larry Lee has. Now I'll shut off the computer, so nobody knows we were here."

Chris held out his hands. "Okay, link hands. And remember, you're only invisible; people can still hear you, so don't talk or yelp or anything."

"How about sneezing?" Jessica asked. Chris was about to forbid that when he realized she was just joking.

"Okay," he said. "Now . . . *To-bira-re!*" It was the same spell that Chrissie had used earlier to make herself invisible, but with Redfire and Chris to help, it was a lot more powerful this time. Everybody vanished from view, but she could feel the grip of Chris and Henry, so she knew they were still there.

"This is major weird," Henry's voice said from the air. "But stellar cool."

"Okay, let's head for the door," Chrissie said. "Quiet once it's open!"

She walked across the carpet, which helped to deaden any sound they might be making. Chris stopped at the door and then the handle turned slowly. It was bizarre seeing the door inch open.

"Okay," Chris whispered back. "We're clear to go. We'll stay close to the wall, since most people walk down the middle of a corridor. Henry, you'd better lead, since you studied the map."

There was a short delay while Henry took the lead, and Chrissie now held Jessica's hand along with Chris's. Then a short jerk from Chris got her moving. They halted just a moment outside so that Jessica could close the door behind them, and then Henry led the way. They went through the outer office, which must be for the secretary, only that

was just as empty as Larry Lee's. The door
there led to a busy corridor.

It was really weird, walking like this.
Chrissie could feel the hands of Chris and
Jessica, but saw absolutely nothing of them
or Henry. They stuck close to the wall, moving very slowly. People in a hurry rushed by,
but, as Chris said, most stuck to the center of
the corridor.

Then there were two secretaries ahead,
lounging by the wall, holding papers and talking. Henry hesitated, and then led them to
the opposite wall. Jessica, unable to see her
feet, almost stumbled and fell. One of the
women blinked, puzzled at the slight noise,
but then went on talking. Chrissie breathed
again.

It was slow going, but they made their way
to the restricted doorway, which was in a
short corridor with no other doorways off it.
That made things simpler, since there
weren't any passersby. Nor, thankfully, was
there any sign of a guard. Larry Lee obviously
trusted his computers more than he trusted
people.

But there was a problem. Henry coughed
quietly and tapped the entrance machinery

gently. "Infrared scanner," he said softly. "Does our being invisible make us invisible to that?"

Chris sighed. "I don't even know what it is, so I doubt it," his voice answered.

"Body heat," Henry said.

"Oh. Then it will pick us up, I guess," Chris confessed. "I only disguised us from being seen."

Henry thought for a minute. "I hope it doesn't matter," he finally said. "We'll be using our passes to get in, so the computer should expect to pick up four people."

"But what if there's somebody monitoring the computer inside?" Chrissie asked. "They'll expect to see four people enter, won't they?"

"There's nobody out here," Henry pointed out. "I don't think there will be anybody watching things inside, either."

"But you can't be sure," Jessica muttered.

"No, I can't," Henry agreed. "We're taking a chance. But we don't have much choice, do we?"

"No," Chrissie agreed. "Okay, let's see what happens."

Henry held out his pass. Now that it wasn't

in his pocket, it became visible. He swiped it through the reader and then walked to the door. If it couldn't see his body heat because of the spell, they wouldn't be able to get inside. And it might even sound an alarm. Chrissie held her breath.

The door opened, and she smiled. She went next, and the other two followed.

The corridor they were in now was very short, and it was glowing. Henry must have known that they were worried. "Some sort of decontamination," he explained. "Just to make sure we don't take any dust or bugs in with us. It won't harm us."

"I'm glad to hear that," Redfire muttered.

The door at the end of the room opened, and they all stepped through it. Then Chrissie walked into Chris, who was stopped dead.

There was a security guard staring right at them.

chapter
TEN

Chrissie had to hold back the gasp she wanted to make. There was no mistaking the fact that he was staring right at them, because of the shocked expression on his face. Then he glanced down at the computer panel in front of him as if he couldn't believe his eyes. She realized what the problem was immediately—he could see four people on the infrared device, and nobody at all with his eyes. It would only be a matter of seconds before he sounded the alarm. What could she do?

Maybe Redfire could use his power of persuasion to stop the guard? But the man's hand was already moving toward what had to be the alarm button. Chrissie didn't have time to think about it. She just yelled out: *"To-roga-re!"* *Don't move!*

Immediately the man froze where he was, halfway through his gesture, his hand hovering over the alarm button. He looked panicked but frozen solid.

"Good thinking," Chris said approvingly from the air. "Kara, how long will that spell last?"

"About fifteen minutes," the dragon answered. "Chrissie's power reserves are running down. She needs to recharge herself soon, or her magic will stop altogether."

"That's not long," Chrissie said, worried. "As soon as he recovers, he's going to sound the alarm."

"If he can," Chris replied. The guard's pass badge suddenly floated off his shirt and onto the computer. "If we work together, we can move him into that side room there and then lock the door. Without his pass, he can't get out again."

It was difficult working together when they couldn't see one another, but the four of them managed to pick the guard up between them and carry him to a small room. Then they closed and locked the door.

"That should buy us a bit more time," Chris decided.

"You're going to need it," Redfire warned them all. "Your invisibility spell is going to wear off in about two minutes."

"Then let's hurry," Chrissie said. "Henry, you take the lead again. Let's hope we can make it to this matter transporter room before we turn visible."

"It's not far," Henry assured them, taking her hand. "This way."

Luckily, since this was a restricted area, there weren't many other people around. They only passed two on their trip to the forbidden room. They made it just in time. They were just inside the room with the door closed when they all suddenly became visible again.

"That was close," Chris muttered.

"Oh, wow!" Henry breathed out as he looked around the room they were in. Chrissie had to agree with him—this place was impressive. It was like a set from a science-fiction movie.

The walls were lined with computers and other machines, all buzzing and clicking away, with their lights flashing in odd patterns. TV screens had pictures and words rushing across them faster than she could read. In the center of the room was what had to be the matter transmitter itself. It was about twenty feet tall and resembled a metal igloo that had been badly wired for cable TV. There were dishes and wires and long, thin rods sticking out at all angles.

"Well, it looks like they have *something* here that works," Jessica said. "Are you sure it can't be a matter transmitter?"

Henry didn't seem sure of anything. "I've got to check it out." He ran to the closest of the computers and started typing away.

Redfire sniffed and was puzzled. "There's a stink of magic in here," he announced. "And it's not coming from either of you."

Chrissie was puzzled. "It looks like Larry Lee has managed to use magic, after all," she said. "But how can that be?"

"I don't know," Chris answered. "But Redfire's right—I can feel some other magic in here." He started to walk around the room but stopped suddenly in front of a computer behind the igloo. "This is it," he decided. "It's coming from here."

"A computer?" Chrissie shook her head. "How can a computer produce magic?"

"It can't," Henry said. "And it isn't. It's just tapping into an energy source."

"I don't understand," Chris complained.

Chrissie did, though. "It's like when Lori Lee managed to control those Elementals on your world," she explained. "Larry Lee is doing the same thing here. Somehow, he must have found a way to control magic coming into this world by means of his supercomputers, and he's using it to make this impossible machine work."

Chris suddenly got it. "He must have broken through the barriers that separate my world from yours," he realized. "He's drawing magic from my Earth." He sounded very worried.

"Is that a bad thing?" Jessica asked.

"It could be," Chris said grimly. "It will drain magic that my world needs."

"Like a battery," Chrissie realized. "If you use it too much, it runs down."

Chris looked puzzled, not knowing what a battery was. "If Larry Lee is using magic in *this* world, then it's coming from my world, and the Law of Conservation of Magic might break down."

"The what?" asked Jessica.

"It's like energy in this world," Henry said. "There's a law stating that energy can't be lost or gained, just changed. I imagine the same is true for magic in your world?"

"Yes, exactly," Chris agreed. "It doesn't matter how much we use in our world, there's always a constant amount. But if magic is used in *this* world, it drains it away from mine. If enough is drained away, then we won't be able to do magic anymore."

Chrissie felt a stabbing pain of guilt. "Then every time I use magic in this world, it drains it away from yours?"

"Or if I do it here," Chris agreed. "But that's nothing to worry about. We use only a tiny bit of the magic, but this machine—it's using *lots* of magic. Every time it switches on, I'll bet there's a measurable magical drain from my world."

"Then we've really got to stop Larry Lee," Jessica said. "Not just to stop him from ruling our world, but also so he won't ruin yours."

"Yes," Chris agreed.

"Right." Chrissie was thinking fast. "Look, if he's draining magic from your world, doesn't that mean that there's got to be some sort of hole in your world? And if that's the case, can't you get someone there to find it and block it?"

"It's worth a try," Chris agreed. "But that means we have to get a message across to somebody who'll believe us and do something."

"What about Samantha?" Chrissie suggested. She was Chris's older sister, and Chrissie liked and trusted her a lot.

"I can't do it," he apologized. "I can only call up somebody in a mirror if their opposite is here with us. Since you and I are here together, it has to be either Henry's or Jessica's twin."

"Mine, I guess," Henry said. "If she's like me, she's a dweeb, but people will listen to her."

"Uh, yes," Chris agreed. "Okay, let's go find a mirror or glass somewhere and do the spell."

"While you do that, Jessica and I will look around," Chrissie said. "Maybe we can find out where Larry Lee has gone. We can't have much time left now." Chris and Henry hurried off to contact Hannah Plunkett on the other world. Chrissie and Jessica wandered around the room, trying to find anything to help them.

Chrissie knew she wouldn't get anywhere like that. It was all computers, and computers were Henry's gift, not hers. But as they prowled, she did hear a loud humming sound, and then something clanging. She glanced at the big metal igloo. Several of the dishes were moving, and there was a bluish glow around a number of the rods.

"Uh, guys," she called out. "I think this thing is being used. . . ."

Henry and Chris came hurrying over, their emergency message finished. Henry blinked through his glasses at the computer by the device. "Yes," he agreed. "There's something coming through. We had better be invisible or something when they reach here."

Chris shook his head. "We can't go invisible again for at least an hour," he said. "Spells can't be piled up like that. We'd better hide."

"Where?" asked Jessica, gesturing.

She was right; there was absolutely nowhere in the room for them to hide. The computers lined the walls, with no gaps behind them. And the only other thing in the room was the transporter.

The lights started to flash, and there was the sound of a door opening.

They were trapped!

chapter ELEVEN

And then Chris called out a magical spell: *"To-tama!" Be small!*

There was a delicious shudder through her whole body, and then Chrissie became giddy, almost falling. It was as if the room had expanded a hundred times. Walls shot up, computer panels became immense, and the floor she was standing on was no longer smooth. It was suddenly terribly uneven. When her head cleared, Chrissie seemed to be only half an inch tall.

"Let's get out of here!" Chris yelled. "We're so small, somebody might crush us if they stepped on us!"

Chrissie realized that this was quite true:

Nobody looked at the bugs under their feet, and they were now no bigger than insects. The four of them hurried to huddle beside the doorway to the metal igloo. Her heart was pounding—she'd only gone about six feet, but it felt like half a mile because of her size. Panting, she leaned against the wall and waited.

The door opened, and a dozen huge people stepped out of the igloo. Four of them were dressed like soldiers; the other eight were in shirtsleeves and white pants. Two of these were women with short hair. All eight looked worried and very cross.

"I don't know how you managed this," one of the men, who was an astronaut, said. "But you can't get away with hijacking a space shuttle."

"We just did," one of the soldiers answered. "And there's nothing that you can do about it. You're stuck here on Earth now, and our crew has taken over."

"So that's it!" Chrissie exclaimed, knowing her tiny voice could never be heard by the huge people. "Larry Lee didn't have a spy on the shuttle—he used this transporter to beam himself and some soldiers up, and they took over the whole thing, and sent the eight astronauts back here."

"Right," agreed Henry. "And I'll bet that's where he is right now. He'll want to be on the spot when his plan to take over the world works."

"It hasn't worked yet," Chris said grimly. "We can still beat him."

"At this size," Redfire reminded him, "you couldn't beat a fly. Larry Lee wouldn't even notice you."

That was a good point. "How long will this spell last?" Chrissie asked the firedrake.

"About another two minutes. Chris's magic is getting weaker, too."

Oh, wonderful! Chrissie looked at the huge people. The soldiers were marching the astronauts out the main door. "They must be intending to hold them prisoner somewhere," she reasoned. "That will keep them out of here for a while. It gives us a chance now."

"To do what?" Jessica asked.

"To get to the space shuttle," Chrissie decided. "Henry, do you think you could operate this machine?"

"Once I'm back to normal, I think I could," he replied. "The machine must still be set for the space shuttle, so we just need to reverse the direction to get there. But what do we do when we're there?"

"What we've done so far," Chrissie answered. "Make it up as we go along. What else can we do?"

"I'd suggest looking out for trouble," Redfire commented. He pointed with one claw. "Like right there."

They all looked around. Jessica screamed, and Chrissie shivered with shock.

There was an immense spider striding across the floor toward them. Despite the fact that this was supposed to be a sterile room, this monstrous spider had managed to get in. It was probably really a tiny creature, maybe half an inch across normally. But *they* were now only half an inch tall, and this thing was the size of a very, very large dog to them. It was all hair and eyes—except for the mouth. There were large mandibles that were opening and closing, looking for food, and the spider was drooling.

"I think it thinks we're lunch," Chris said nervously.

"I think we could be," Chrissie answered, her mouth dry with fear. The horrible mon-

ster was stalking them now, obviously thinking they were some new, delicious sort of
insects. "Jessica, Henry—you'd better stay
behind us. Chris and I are the only ones with
magic."

"Not for long," Kara said. "You're both
pretty much on the edge right now. And the
more magic you use, the faster you'll run
down."

"We don't have a lot of choice," Chrissie
replied, but she was talking a lot braver than
she felt. She had no idea how they could fight
off this spider, but it shouldn't have to be for
long. The shrinking spell *must* wear off soon!

Without warning the spider attacked. It
leaped, using all eight of its legs to propel
itself, its mandibles wide, ready to rip into a
victim. Chrissie ducked, and yelled: *"Divas,
to-nikta!" Fire, appear!* Immediately she held
a ball of blazing flames in her right hand.
Amazingly, it didn't burn her, even though
she could feel the heat from it. She pitched it
like a baseball right at the spider.

The monster twisted in midair, and the
fireball went sailing past it. But the twist had
ruined the spider's aim, and it missed the four
tiny people. But it was moving so quickly

that it was almost upon them before Chrissie could react.

"Ha!" screamed Henry, rushing forward. Chrissie saw that he'd found a bent paper clip on the floor. He was gripping the rounded edge and using the bent end like a sword, stabbing at the spider with it. It was a terribly brave act, and Chrissie felt very proud of him. She was also scared for him because the spider had just reared up on its back legs, and Henry's charge missed it completely. The spider stabbed down with one leg, pinning Henry to the floor. Slavering, the creature bent forward to bite off its victim's head.

Then it was Chris's turn to throw a blazing globe of fire. This time, though, the spider didn't move out of the way in time because it was so intent on its food. The fireball hit it on the back, igniting the dark hairs there. The spider screamed and reared up. That gave Chrissie and Jessica the seconds they needed to grab Henry's arms and pull him away from the monster.

The spider was in pain, though the fire died out quickly. Chrissie tried to conjure up another fireball herself, but all she managed was a pathetic little fizzling flame.

Her magic had run out completely. . . .

She snatched up the paper clip instead, holding it out to keep the spider at bay, but it didn't work. One of the spider's legs lashed out, catching the clip and sending it spinning from her hand.

"My magic's all gone!" Chris wailed as he dashed forward, trying to help. But he wasn't fast enough. The spider pounced, using its legs to pin Chrissie to the floor.

Stunned, she couldn't move. She could only look up into that monstrous face. The huge eyes stared down at her, and the mouth worked in anticipation of a large meal. The jaws opened and closed, ready to tear her head off.

And then, dizzyingly fast, she was her normal size again. Her head spun, but not as fast as the now-terrified spider. It couldn't understand why its meal was gone and an immense human was in its place. It jumped off her—

And right under Chris's foot. He stomped down with satisfaction. "Serves it right," he said.

Chrissie was glad that the danger was over, but she did feel Chris had been a bit harsh, since the spider couldn't hurt them now. Still, the spider was now the least of their worries. They were back to normal, but neither she nor Chris had any magic left. And they still had to try to stop Larry Lee.

Henry blinked and pushed his glasses back up his nose. "That was close," he gasped. "I suppose I'd better check to be sure I can really work this matter transmitter." He went to the computers and started typing.

"Do you think those soldiers will come back?" Jessica asked.

"I don't know," Chrissie confessed. "I hope not. If we can just stop Larry Lee in time . . ."

"But how?" asked Chris. "Without our magic, we don't have much to work with."

"We have our brains," Chrissie said firmly. "That's how we defeated Lori Lee, after all. She had stronger magic than we did, but we were smarter. We have to act the same with Larry Lee."

"Easier said than done," Jessica muttered.

"You don't have to come," Chrissie told her.

"What sort of a friend would I be if I didn't stick with you?" asked Jessica. "And I don't think I could talk you into staying, could I?"

"No," Chrissie admitted. "We have to finish this now."

"Then I'm coming, too." Jessica stuck her chin out and folded her arms. She could be very stubborn when she wanted to, and Chrissie was glad she was her friend.

"Okay," Henry said, joining them again. "I've set the controls. They're really simple, thank goodness. All we have to do is to go inside the machine, close the door, and hit the start button. That will send us up into space on the shuttle."

"You could stay here, you know," Chrissie told him.

Henry looked offended. "And miss the chance to be one of the first kids in space? No way! They'll be *so* jealous of me in the Science Club after this. If they believe a word of it, that is."

Well, that seemed to settle it, then. Chrissie's mouth was dry again, and she knew she was scared. But she also knew she *had* to go through with this. "Right," she decided. "Let's go."

They marched through the open door and into the metal igloo. It was about eight feet across and the same height inside. Henry found the control panel and closed the door. It *hissed* shut with a rather final sound.

Henry's fingers halted by the Transmit button.

"Are we all ready?" he asked.

"No," Redfire replied. "But nobody ever listens to my complaints, do they?"

"No," Chris agreed. "Okay, Henry—let's do it."

Henry nodded. His finger stabbed out and triggered the button.

There was a wave of tingling all through Chrissie's body as the transmitter started up. It was like a mild electrical shock, working swiftly from her toes to the ends of her hair.

Then there was no weight at all to her body, and she was floating.

chapter TWELVE

Chrissie screamed as her feet left the ground and she fell over backward. She didn't hit anything, though. Instead, she just floated in midair.

The others were floating, too, just as confused and shaken as she was.

They were on the space shuttle, that was obvious. There were lots of storage lockers and hand-grips and computer panels all around them. There was a tiny window on the far side of the small room they were floating in, and out of it Chrissie could see a black sky sprinkled with bright points of stars. Kara was holding on to Chrissie very tightly to avoid floating away. The tiny dragon popped down the front of her T-shirt, where she obviously felt safer. Redfire had vanished in a similar manner.

"Zero gravity!" Henry gasped. "Of course, we're in Earth orbit. There's no gravity to hold us down." He was struggling and twisting in the air, floating gently. Then he grabbed one of the straps and pulled himself to the wall. Once he was there, he was able to grab hold of Chrissie's ankle. Since there wasn't any gravity, it was pretty easy for him to pull her by the ankle to join him. Together they caught the other two. A moment later, panting, they were all clinging onto the straps for dear life and shaking.

"I feel sick," Jessica complained.

"Don't throw up," Henry warned her. "Without gravity, it will just float in the air and make the room really smell bad. And if we move, we might run into it."

"I feel even sicker after you told me that," Jessica said. "That's disgusting."

Henry shrugged. "It's just science."

"It makes me love magic more," Chris decided. "Well, we seem to be in this space shuttle of yours, I guess."

"Definitely," Henry agreed.

"Then where is everybody?" Chris wanted to know.

"On duty, I should think," Henry answered. "This is the sleeping and experiment area. Larry Lee's men came in here, knowing the crew would be at the controls. So the invaders could get in without being spotted. And that means so can we."

"Except Larry Lee's men had guns when they came," Chrissie pointed out. "We don't have anything, not even magic."

"Well," Kara said. "You were warned. Mind you—"

Chris ignored the dragon. "Henry, can't you do something? You're the scientist in the group."

Henry looked both pleased and scared. "Well, I *am* a genius," he said humbly, "but I'm afraid piloting a space shuttle is a bit out of my reach just yet. I don't have a clue what any of the controls do."

"Can't we cut off the power somehow?" Chrissie suggested. "Then Larry Lee won't be able to take over the satellites."

Henry shook his head quickly. "No way. If we shut down the power, we'll shut down the air and the heat. There's neither of those in space, so without the power to the shuttle, we'd choke to death and then freeze solid. I *really* think we need a different suggestion."

"Couldn't we just break something?" Jessica offered. "You know, a radio dish or something? So he can't control the satellites?"

"You little vandal you," Chrissie said, grinning. "But how would we know which one to break? If Henry doesn't know, how would we?"

"Well, we can't just do *nothing*," Chris growled. "We've come all this way. There must be *something* we can do."

"Of course there is," said a new voice. "You can put up your hands."

Chrissie looked around, and her body twisted as well. In the doorway stood a soldier.

They'd been captured before they could do anything. . . .

"Uh, if we put up our hands, we'll float away," Henry pointed out.

The man obviously hadn't thought about that. He considered a moment. "Well, you're just a bunch of kids anyway. You're no real danger. Though I don't know how you managed to get here."

"We're a lot smarter than you think," Chrissie said. She was scared, but she wasn't going to let the man insult them.

"If you were really smart, you wouldn't be here," the soldier snapped. He reached into a locker and pulled out several pair of what looked like sandals. "Put these on," he ordered, tossing the sandals in their direction.

It wasn't easy to catch them using only one hand, but because there wasn't any gravity the sandals didn't fall to the ground. In fact, it was impossible to tell which way was up or down for that matter. All directions seemed the same. Chrissie managed to pull on the sandals eventually, though they were several sizes too big, since they were made for adults.

"Okay, there's Velcro on the soles," the soldier informed them. "And there are Velcro strips all over the walls. Using them, you can walk almost normally. So get started and come with me. Mr. Lee will want to see you all."

Chrissie stepped onto one of the patches and felt her foot catch hold. It took her a few tries to get used to it, because she had to make sure that one foot was anchored in place before she could lift the other. But eventually she got the hang of it, and was able to walk across the room to stand beside the soldier. The other three followed. It looked funny, as if they were walking in mud, but it worked.

"Crazy kids," the soldier muttered. "Well, you've asked for trouble, and now you've got it. Go through there." He pointed to the far door, which was open now, and Chrissie could hear voices and lots of electronic sounds.

She walked through the small room and then went through the doorway. She gasped.

They were on the flight deck of the space shuttle. There were four people in chairs, all bent over their instrument panels and talking into microphones and adjusting instruments. There were several windows in the room, looking out into space. Half of the view was taken up with the bright and glowing Earth. It was so huge they could only see a small piece of it—directly above them. The shuttle felt as if it was upside-down!

Three of the people ignored them, but one man stared at them in astonishment. "*They* are the intruders?" he asked. He was obviously Larry Lee. He looked just like Lori Lee had, with pale white hair, icy-looking skin, and dark, dark eyes. His space uniform was all white, too, even his Velcro sandals.

"Yes, Mr. Lee," the soldier agreed. "Four kids. I don't know how they got here."

"The same way we did, obviously," Larry Lee snapped. "Via our matter transmitter." His eyes narrowed as he stared at them. "What do you think you're doing, going on a field trip or something?"

"We came to stop you from taking over the ELEMENT satellites," Chrissie said. "We know what you're up to."

"Do you indeed?" Larry Lee laughed and stroked back his neat white hair. "You know, I was expecting the FBI, or maybe the Marines. But *four kids?* It's so funny, it's pathetic. What do you imagine you can do?"

"I don't know," Chrissie admitted. "But we won't let you take over the world. You're an evil man."

"Of *course* I am," he agreed. "I've worked hard at it. I've spent *years* acting nice. It was so hard, and it feels so good to be bad now. We all need a dream to work toward, don't you agree? Mine is to rule the world, and I'm only a few minutes away from achieving my dream. Normally, I like kids as much as the next man—especially if the next man is Attila the Hun—but you four have really annoyed me. How did you get here?"

"We broke into your headquarters," Henry informed him. "And then used your matter transporter to come here."

"Belmont!" Larry Lee yelled in a very angry voice.

One man looked around. "Yes, sir?"

"What kind of morons do we have working as security guards?" the would-be ruler snarled. "Four kids just walked into the heart of our business and beamed themselves up here. You're not going to get your Christmas bonus if you keep up this shoddy work!"

"I'm very sorry, Mr. Lee," Belmont apologized. "I'll look into it when we get back and make absolutely certain that it won't happen again."

"It had better not," Larry Lee growled. "Next time we'll be invaded by kindergartners!" He turned back to Chrissie and her friends. "So, now that you're here," he purred, "what do you plan to do?"

"We don't know," Jessica admitted miserably. "We just hoped we could find the satellite controls and stop you from using them."

Larry Lee was obviously astonished, and then he broke out into laughter. "Oh, I needed that," he gasped. "It was time for a good laugh. You don't have a clue what you're doing, do you?"

"No," Chrissie admitted miserably.

"Well, allow me to show you what you're looking for," he answered. He gestured at the panel in front of him. "This is the satellite master control," he explained. It appeared to be very complicated, with all sorts of controls, dials, screens, and buttons. There was a keyboard to type in commands. "I will control the ELEMENT system from here in exactly"—he looked at a ticking clock—"five and a half minutes. It's going to be a lot of fun taking over the world. Normally I'd invite you to stay and watch and maybe cheer me on as I win. But, as you can see, things are kind of busy. Stark!"

"Sir!" The soldier saluted him.

"Take these children for a walk, will you? Somewhere nice and quiet—like out of the nearest airlock." He grinned at Chrissie and her friends. "It's what they always did to pirates," he said. "Make them walk the plank." He laughed. "Only you've got a long way to fall. But don't worry—you'll suffocate long before you burn up when you hit the Earth's atmosphere."

Chrissie went white with shock. "You can't mean it?" she gasped.

"Oh, yes I can. This will teach you not to poke your noses into my business." Larry Lee laughed again. "Of course, you won't live long enough to profit by the lesson, but you can't have everything. And in about two minutes you won't have anything. Especially life." And he laughed again, long and hard.

chapter THIRTEEN

Belmont, the man at the pilot's controls, twisted around. "Surely you can't mean that, Mr. Lee?" he asked, shocked. "They're just *children.*"

"They're *annoying* children," Larry Lee answered. "And if I don't deal with them now, they'll grow up to become even more annoying adults. I'm doing the world a favor by disposing of them." He scowled. "If you have a problem with that, I'm afraid I'll have to fire you."

Belmont swallowed, and considered. Then he turned back to the controls.

"You have to be strict with your employees," Larry Lee informed Chrissie. "Otherwise discipline goes to pieces." He looked at the soldier. "I told you to take these kids and throw them out of the airlock. And I mean *now*. Unless you want me to get somebody else to do it, and have you join them?"

"No, sir!" the man barked. He gestured at the four kids. "Come on, Mr. Lee is a very busy man."

"*Busy* isn't the word I'd use to describe him," Chrissie muttered. Still, she had no choice but to obey the man. Chris, Henry, and Jessica, all pale, followed. The soldier closed the door to the cabin behind them.

"That way," he said, gesturing toward the back of the shuttle.

"You can't *seriously* intend to do what he said, can you?" Jessica pleaded. "We're just kids. You can't kill us."

"It's not up to me, miss," the man answered. "I'm just obeying orders."

"It *is* up to you," Chris said firmly. "You could refuse to do what that lunatic told you."

"Mr. Lee will be running everything in less than five minutes," the soldier said. "If I don't obey him, he will have me shot."

"Is that the sort of man you *want* to be running everything?" Chrissie asked him. "Why don't you help us stop him?"

For a moment she thought she'd managed to get through to the man, but then he shook his head. "You don't stand a chance against Mr. Lee," he said. "I'll stick with the winning side."

"Even though it means killing us?" Jessica asked bitterly.

"I'm a soldier," the man said. "I do what I'm told. I'm not responsible for my orders."

"Yes, you are," Chris informed him. "And you will have to answer for them."

They had reached the airlock. The soldier pointed once again as he opened the first door. "Inside, now."

"No. I won't go," Chrissie said, crossing her arms and standing still.

The man sighed. "Either you walk in, or I'll break one of your legs and your friends will have to carry you in," he said. He tensed his hands, ready for a karate chop. Chrissie could see that he meant what he was saying. She had no choice.

Walking into the airlock was one of the

most terrifying things she had ever done. But she refused to let the soldier see how scared she was. She just hoped it wasn't too obvious. Chris, Henry, and Jessica—on the verge of tears—all followed her, and then the door slammed. There was the hiss of its being sealed.

"We're going to die!" Jessica howled. "We'll be pulled back to Earth and die!"

"Don't be silly," Henry snapped. "We'll die a lot sooner than that. When the air is pumped out of this airlock, the outer door will open, and we'll be pushed out into space. We'll have nothing to breathe, and we'll die in thirty seconds."

"You're a real comfort," Chris muttered. He sounded as scared as Chrissie was. He obviously couldn't think of any way out of this, either.

"Is it my imagination," Jessica asked, her voice shaking, "or is it getting hard to breathe?"

"The air is being pumped out," Henry answered. "It's not your imagination."

Kara opened an eye. "Now would be a very good time to do something," she commented to Chrissie.

"What?" Chrissie asked. Her throat was starting to hurt, and it was getting harder to fill her lungs. "Our magic ran out, remember?"

Kara shrugged. "Then it's a good job I replenished it, isn't it?"

"What?" Chrissie was stunned. Was it true? Did she have her magic back? She turned her thoughts inward and felt the tingle of magic in her body. Yes! Somehow she had her powers back!

"Todor, to-nikta!" she said quickly. *Air, appear!* Immediately she could breathe properly again, and she felt a flood of relief. She'd created a bubble of air surrounding all four of them.

"I don't know what you did," Henry said gratefully, "but you'd better think about heating us up, too. The door's about to open, and it's *really* cold in space."

"To-chara!" Chris said quickly, and it was as if they were wrapped in soft, woolen blankets to keep them warm.

And then the airlock door opened.

Chrissie and the others grabbed one another by the hands as they were shot out of the airlock into space. For a second Chrissie was terrified that they were going to die despite their magic, but then she realized that they were warm and could still breathe.

Then shock set in as she stared up. The Earth was right over their heads, huge and glowing. She watched clouds being blown across the oceans, and part of Africa came into view below the clouds.

All the rest of the area was taken up with pitch-black space and the bright gleam of tiny stars.

"Cool!" Henry said in awe. "First kids to do a space walk."

"Space *float*," Jessica corrected him. She pointed back the way they had come. "We're getting farther and farther away from the space shuttle, guys."

"Not to worry. Now that we have our magic we can fix everything," Chris said. Then he frowned. "But I don't understand how we got it back."

"Of course you don't," Redfire said, rolling his eyes. "That's because you don't pay attention. Kara and I did it."

"But *how?*" asked Chrissie. "We were completely out, and we didn't go back to Chris's world to get a fresh charge."

"You didn't have to," Kara said. "Look, that matter transmitter machine of Larry Lee's is powered by magic. We just drained a bit of that and gave it to you. You've had your powers back ever since we went through that machine."

"Oh." Chrissie had completely forgotten about the machine tapping into the magic world. Thank goodness the dragon and firedrake hadn't!

"Well, if you've got your powers back," Henry said, grinning devilishly, "then I think it's about time we went and settled the score with Larry Lee."

"I couldn't agree more," Chrissie admitted. She was really psyched for this. It was payback time for Larry Lee! *"To-ava!"* Return! Immediately they stopped drifting away from the now-tiny shuttle and shot back through space toward it.

As they reached the nose of the shuttle, Chris said: *"To-nama!"* Be fluid! They slipped straight through the wall of the shuttle and stepped right into the control cabin.

It was hard to tell who was the most astonished to see them. Belmont screamed and almost jumped out of his seat. Larry Lee just appeared shocked, his hands poised over the controls.

"Right," Chrissie said grimly. "You've made us mad, and that was a *serious* mistake!"

chapter

FOURTEEN

"I don't know how you managed that trick," Larry Lee said, "but you're too late to stop me. ELEMENT is mine. I only need to send the commands to the satellites, and they're under my control." He reached for the keyboard to begin his takeover of the world.

"Try it," Chrissie snapped. She'd been thinking up this spell on the way back. *"To-nikta-re!" Disappear!*

The whole panel vanished as Larry Lee stared at it.

Chrissie grinned. "You can't type on what you can't see," she informed him. "You're not taking over anything, I promise you that."

"You interfering brats!" Larry Lee yelled. He turned to the soldier. "Get them!"

The soldier hesitated, apparently unsure what to do, and definitely unsure what was happening.

Redfire uncurled, emerging from his hiding place inside Chris's T-shirt and showing himself for the first time. He was only a small firedrake, but even that was quite impressive. "I wouldn't do that if I were you," he said. It was probably the fact that the animal was talking that made the soldier shake so much.

It didn't scare Larry Lee, though. He gave a snarl of anger and started to get up from his seat. Chrissie had no doubt that he'd do his own dirty work—if he could.

"*To-sepa!*" she growled, gesturing at Larry Lee. *Be stuck!* No matter how he struggled, he couldn't get out of his seat. That would keep him out of trouble for a while.

"These kids are serious trouble," Belmont complained, shaking. "How can they do all of this?"

"Magic," Henry answered with a grin. "Maybe I should change you into a rat? Oh, sorry, you already are one." Belmont went pale, not knowing, of course, that Henry didn't have any idea how to do magic. And he didn't have a partner, like Kara, to help out.

"It's time you all surrendered," Chris called out to the crew. "Larry Lee's crazy plot isn't going to work. He's going to jail, and all of you with him. If you give up now, we won't have to do anything to you."

"I'm never giving up!" Larry Lee snarled. "I'll kill all of you! You won't stop me!"

"Wow," Jessica said, amused. "He sounds like a real movie villain, doesn't he? All he needs is a big white cat to stroke." She'd gotten all of her courage back, Chrissie noted.

"But he's still nasty," Chrissie pointed out. "I think we're going to have to fix him once and for all."

"Uh, what are we going to do?" Chris asked her in a whisper. "I don't think we can get this whole space shuttle thing back to where it belongs. Even though we've got our magic back, it isn't *that* strong."

Chrissie hadn't actually thought about that. "How about we zap Larry Lee straight to jail?" she whispered back.

"I don't know where the jails are on your world," he answered. "And he's not actually been arrested for anything, so the police might just let him out again."

That was a problem. But they had to do *something* . . .

"*To-roga-re!*" Chris called. *Don't move!* It had worked on the guard on Earth, and it worked up in space, too. Everybody but the four of them was stopped dead. "Right," Chris said. "That should give us some time to think this out. Redfire, how long will they be frozen stiff?"

"About ten minutes," the firedrake answered. "Which should give you plenty of time to decide what to do about *that.*"

"About *what?*" Chris asked. Then he, Chrissie, and the rest turned to look out of the shuttle's main window, where the firedrake was pointing.

Directly ahead of them was a strange, whirlpool-like effect. It was larger than the shuttle, and spinning in place. It was all red and gold and purples, with flashes of electric blue lightning. They were getting closer and closer to it.

"What is that?" Chrissie asked Henry, scared.

"I don't know," he confessed, gulping. "It's no astronomical event I've ever heard about. I don't know *what* can be causing it."

"Magic is," Kara snapped.

"Hannah came through," Chris said as he started to understand. "She must have got the authorities on my world to believe her story, and now they're taking back all the magic from this world again."

Chrissie swallowed. "Uh . . . *we* have magic from your world, Chris," she pointed out. "If they're draining it back, won't that drain us again?"

"Oh, right . . ." He looked worried. "That thing is a vortex of some sort that leads to limbo," he realized. "It's sucking the shuttle into it." He checked. "We don't have enough magic between us to pull us back out of it again, I'm afraid. The only thing we can do is not be here when the shuttle is sucked up."

"Guys," Henry said firmly. "Now would be a *very* good time to leave."

"Definitely," Chris agreed. *"To-ava!"* he cried loudly. *Return!*

Chrissie saw the great vortex right in front

of the ship. Lightning continued to flash soundlessly, since there was no air in space to carry noise. The shuttle was being drawn right into it.

Then all at once Chrissie felt a tingle in her body, and she knew she wasn't in the shuttle any longer.

chapter
FIFTEEN

"I was wondering when you'd get back," said a very familiar voice.

Chrissie looked around. They'd arrived in the metal igloo back in Dallas. Well, Chris *had* said for them to return, and this was where they had launched themselves into space. Sitting by the door, delicately licking one paw, was Bellwether.

"I might have known you'd show up," Chris said with a sigh. "Are you causing trouble again?"

"Me?" Bellwether managed to sound shocked. "Never." He held up a paw solemnly. "I'm a reformed cat. I was just waiting here to make sure you got back all right."

"What? You were going to come looking for us if we didn't?" Chris asked sarcastically.

"I hadn't quite decided what I would do," the cat announced. "But I certainly don't plan to stay around here any longer. It's getting very noisy. I'll catch you all later."

"What does he mean?" asked Jessica.

"Who knows?" Chris replied. "He's not a very honest cat, whatever he says." And Bellwether was already gone. "Still, maybe we should follow him." Chris led the way out of the matter transporter and back into the control room. All of the computers there seemed to be dead. "What's happened?"

"All of the power's gone," Henry decided. "Hannah shut off the power drain on your world, so now the transmitter won't work."

"That's a good thing," Chrissie said. "I wouldn't trust any of Larry Lee's employees with something like the transmitter. Maybe they're all as bad as he is."

At that moment the door opened and a bunch of people rushed in. They all wore black raincoats and sunglasses, even though they were indoors where it neither rained nor sun shone.

"Oh, no!" Jessica squeaked. "Larry Lee's men!"

"No, miss," one of the men said. He flipped open his wallet to show them a pass. "FBI."

"Cool," Henry said. "Where's Mulder and Scully?"

Chris grinned. "Oh, you watch *The Hex Files*, too, eh?"

"We're the good guys," Chrissie said, sighing with relief. She had thought they were being caught again. "We sent NASA a warning about what Larry Lee was up to."

"You kids?" The FBI agent looked surprised. "How did you manage that?"

Henry grinned. "We're smarter than we look. Are you here to arrest everybody?"

"Everybody but the four of you, it looks like," the man replied. "But how did you get involved in all of this?"

"And do you have any idea where our space shuttle is?" asked one of the astronauts. They had all been freed and had rushed here to try and get back to their ship.

"Ah, well . . ." Chrissie said. "It's a long story."

"Don't worry," the head FBI agent said. "We're really good listeners."

Chrissie sighed. This wasn't going to be neat and tidy, she could tell. There was no simple way to explain about the other world and magic. But there was absolutely no other explanation that would make sense.

She had a terrible feeling that they might still be locked up after all. Only not in a jail but in a mental hospital. . . .

Luckily they were saved from having to explain everything immediately. Other FBI agents turned up, and the astronauts wanted to know how they were going to get back to their shuttle.

"You don't have to worry about that," Henry informed them. "It's not there anymore."

The chief astronaut stared at him. "What? Did Larry Lee blow it up or something?"

"No, not exactly." Henry winced. "It sort of fell through a hole in space."

"And how do you know that?" asked the head FBI man.

"Well, we got off it just in time," Henry said, wilting a bit under their glares.

"And how did you bail out of a space shuttle?" another FBI agent asked. "This so-called matter transmitter stopped working."

"Ah, well, that's sort of hard to explain," Henry admitted. He turned to the others for help. "Come on, guys, don't leave this all to me."

"Why not?" Jessica asked. "You're making such a mess of it already. I for one am quite amused."

"Well, we're not," the FBI agent growled. "You're going to have to come with us and answer lots of questions. I can see it's going to take a few days to get the truth out of you."

Ouch! Chrissie decided that she'd had enough of this. "I really don't think that our explaining anything is going to help anyone," she muttered to Chris. "Particularly us."

"I know what you mean," he agreed. He looked at the FBI man. "Look, we can explain everything, but it has to be in Larry Lee's office."

The FBI head thought a moment, then nodded. "You two, take them up there," he ordered a man and a woman. "Stay with them. I'll be there as soon as I finish up here. Then we'll get to the bottom of things," he warned Chrissie.

"Right," the woman agreed. She looked

quite tough, but gave Chrissie a friendly smile. "Let's get out of here, shall we?"

"Definitely," Chrissie agreed. As they left, they could hear one of the astronauts on a cell phone to NASA.

"What do you mean our shuttle just *vanished*?" he was yelling. "You can't *lose* it! It's our responsibility!" Chrissie had a strong feeling he wasn't going to like the answers he would get.

It was a lot simpler going back to Larry Lee's office since they weren't invisible and didn't need to keep dodging out of everyone's way to avoid being bumped. They still had to do a lot of dodging because there were hundreds of FBI agents leading people in handcuffs or carrying out boxes of papers or computers. They were obviously going to shut down everything Larry Lee had been running.

"We'll catch the head man soon," the FBI woman vowed. "He can't hide forever."

"He might be a bit harder to find than you think," Jessica said, giggling slightly. "He's kind of lost in space."

"He was on the shuttle?" the other agent asked.

"Oh, yes," Jessica agreed.

The FBI woman rolled her eyes. "Well, I don't know how we'll get him back, then. Still, you can tell us all about it soon enough." They had reached Larry Lee's office and went inside. Chrissie was relieved to see that the tatty old carpet from school was still there, on top of Larry Lee's thick, expensive white carpet.

"I'm sure you'll want to know how we got here," Chrissie said. "So we'll have to show you. Come on, everyone." She sat down on the carpet, Chris beside her. Jessica, still giggling a bit, and Henry sat behind them.

"*To-fiva!*" Chris said. *Fly!* The carpet rose off the floor, hovering beside the window. The two FBI agents stared, their faces shocked, their mouths open.

"How do you *do* that?" the woman asked.

"That's nothing," Chris said modestly. "Watch this. *To-nama!*" he ordered the window. *Be fluid!* And then he grinned as the carpet shot through the window and out into the air of Dallas once again.

The two FBI agents yelled, but their voices were cut off as the window went back to being solid again. Chrissie waved back over her shoulder at the agents as the carpet sped away.

"I hope they don't get into trouble for losing us," she said. "Because they'll never find us—all kids look alike to adults. And I definitely think it's better to run away than try to explain everything, don't you?"

"Definitely!" the other three chorused.

chapter SIXTEEN

Back at school Chrissie and the rest slipped the carpet back into the computer room, once again using Chris's don't-look-at-me spell. Redfire made certain that the hall monitors didn't report them.

"Well," Chris said a bit reluctantly, "I guess it's time I went home."

Chrissie nodded. "I think it's about time we all returned to normal."

"I don't know how we can," Jessica said. "Nothing like this has ever happened to me before. It's changed my whole outlook on everything. Magic that *works*." She looked at Chris eagerly. "Do you think *I* could visit your world someday?"

"Who knows?" Chris answered with a big grin. "Stranger things have happened." He looked around. "Like *me* visiting *this* world. It's been a blast, but I think I'll stick to magic, if you don't mind." He stuck out his hand. "Nice to have met you, Jessica, Henry."

"Likewise," Henry replied, pushing his glasses back up on his nose. "This has been quite an incredible day." He grinned. "Space!"

"Yes." Chris smiled. "I can see I'll have to start being nicer to Hannah from now on. Since she's you on my world, it's obvious that I've misjudged her."

"True enough," Chrissie confessed. "I'm really sorry I've been so rotten to you in the past, Henry," she apologized. "We couldn't have stopped Larry Lee without your help."

"Yes," Jessica agreed. "You're not really a dweeb after all."

"Sure I am," Henry answered. "But for a dweeb, I think I'm okay."

"So do we." Chris headed for the closest bathroom. "But I'd better get back now. See you again, I hope. Maybe in less dangerous times."

He hopped back into his own world

through the first mirror. After he waved and the mirror showed only her own reflection, Chrissie felt a bit lost. She liked having Chris around, weird as it was. But it was time to return to normal life now.

Except . . .

She removed Kara from around her neck. "What am I going to do with you?" she asked the little dragon.

"Nothing, I hope," Kara replied. "I was thinking of going back to your bedroom now. I'm *exhausted* from all that magic."

"What do you mean, go back to my bedroom now?" Chrissie scowled at her partner.

"I'll just transport myself back and curl up in bed till you're finished with this silly school business," the dragon explained.

"Transport yourself back?" Chrissie asked slowly.

"Of course." Kara shrugged, rippling her whole body. "Didn't you hear what Chris said? We magical beings can transport to anywhere we've been before."

Chrissie couldn't believe what she was hearing. "You mean you could have just gone home anytime today? Not gotten me in all of that trouble breaking you out?"

"Sure."

"Why didn't you tell me?" she yelled, furious.

"You didn't ask," Kara answered. "Besides, if you're spending all day at school, I wanted to know what the attraction was. I don't understand it myself, so I don't think I'll bother coming again."

"Thank you," growled Chrissie. It didn't help that Jessica and Henry were giggling behind their hands at her.

"You're welcome." Kara paused. "So, how long does this school nonsense go on? A week or two?"

"Till I'm eighteen," Chrissie said with some satisfaction. "Or longer, if I go to college."

Kara looked shocked. "You need rest," she finally decided. "Then maybe you'll wise up. Meanwhile, *I* need rest. See you later." There was a slight *pop* of air as the little dragon vanished. Well, at least that was one less problem. But Chrissie was still annoyed at all the trouble Kara had caused.

Now they had to get back to classes—and explain where they had been. It wasn't going to be easy.

It was worse than she thought. As they left the bathroom, the principal was standing outside, arms crossed, staring at them. "What were you doing in a boys' bathroom, Jessica, Chrissie? And where have you been?" he demanded.

Chrissie winced. It looked like her luck was running true to form—all bad. "Uh . . ." she said, hardly very brightly.

"We were saving the world," Jessica volunteered. "From Larry Lee."

"So you've been listening to the radio, too?" the principal asked. "As you must know, the FBI raided his offices and stopped his nasty little plans. I don't recall hearing anything at all about three schoolchildren being involved."

"Ah, well, sir, you wouldn't," Jessica tried to explain. "They're all too embarrassed to admit it, especially when we took off on a flying carpet and they couldn't stop us. . . ." Her voice trailed off as she saw the principal's stony gaze. "Maybe I should shut up now," she suggested.

A bit late for that, thought Chrissie.

"I don't know whether to give you all detention for skipping classes, or send you to a psychiatrist to have your heads examined," the principal informed them. "But let's start with detention, shall we? Then I can decide about getting your heads shrunk."

Chrissie sighed. It just wasn't *fair*. They'd saved the world, and they were getting detention for it! She wished that Redfire and his ability to persuade people were here, but he was back on his own world. She decided that the very next magical spell she was going to learn would *definitely* have to be how to make people believe what she said.

But she'd have to wait till after detention to learn anything like that.

Dragging their feet, they followed the principal. Some days you just couldn't win.

EPILOGUE

"I think I've finally gotten the space shuttle under some sort of control, sir," Belmont reported from his pilot's seat. "This wherever-we-are is *really* strange, and the controls are a bit funny."

"I'm not interested in excuses," Larry Lee growled. "Just results. We have to get back to Earth somehow."

"That might not be the best idea, sir," Belmont suggested. "After all, with your failure to secure the ELEMENT link, the old authorities are still in power. I'm sure they must know about your plot by now, and the government and the FBI and goodness knows who else must be after us."

Larry Lee just glared at him. "That's it,

Belmont," he snarled. "Just rub in how much we've failed, why don't you? And *think*, you moron! We have only enough air and power in this space shuttle for about a week. If we're not back on Earth by then, we'll *die!* I don't know about you, but dodging the FBI is vastly preferable to dying, you idiot."

"You do have a point, sir," Belmont agreed.

"Of course I do." Larry Lee was pacing up and down angrily. "Now, can you get us back to Earth in that time?"

"I can't honestly say, sir," Belmont answered. "I really don't have much idea where we are right now." He gestured out of the window. Instead of the blackness of space, sprinkled with the brightness of stars, they were flying through some sort of greenish-orange cloud. Lightning was soundlessly flashing all around them. "There doesn't seem to be anything at all out there, sir. There's certainly no sign of Earth. We've entered some sort of space-time . . . thingie."

"Well, if we can get *in*," Larry Lee pointed out, "then we can get *out*. I don't want any of your excuses, just find us a way home."

Belmont sighed. "I'll do my best, sir. Though, as I said—" His voice broke off.

"That's strange," he said, bending over his instruments. "There's something directly ahead of us," he reported.

"Something?" Larry Lee growled. "Can't you be a bit more specific? What sort of something? A planet? A missile? A custard pie?"

"No, it's none of those," Belmont said seriously. "It seems to be . . . a person."

Larry Lee frowned. "I'm not interested in people," he replied. "Ignore it."

"I can't, sir. It seems to be coming toward us."

"In this?" Larry Lee gestured out of the window into the lightning-flecked cloud. "How can anybody be alive out there?"

"I really couldn't say, sir," his assistant replied. "But whoever it is seems to be quite close to us now. Ah, in fact—"

Somebody walked *through* the wall of the shuttle.

"She's here," Belmont finished.

Larry Lee stared in astonishment at the woman, who was staring back at him, just as surprised. She looked almost exactly like himself—long, pure white hair, pale skin, white clothing, and deep black eyes.

"Who are you?" they both asked at the same moment.

"I'm Larry Lee," he replied, walking slowly around her. "Everybody on Earth knows who I am."

"Larry Lee?" The woman thought for a moment, then laughed. "Of course! You're from that silly world where *science* works, aren't you?"

"And you are . . . ?" he asked her.

"Everybody on *my* Earth knows who I am," the woman replied. She stood tall—exactly the same height as Larry Lee himself. "I'm Lori Lee—the greatest magician in my world. I'm your exact opposite."

"You're *me*," Larry Lee said, understanding what she meant. "From another world. You're what I would be there."

"You catch on quickly," Lori Lee agreed. "But you would. After all, you're as brilliant as I am."

"If you're so brilliant," Larry Lee asked her, "why are you in this place, wherever it may be?"

"It's limbo," she answered. "And I was sent here by a bunch of kids."

"A bunch of kids?" he asked, feeling

strange. "They wouldn't happen to have included a blond boy and girl who looked rather alike, would they?"

"They would indeed," Lori Lee agreed. "And, judging from the fact that *you're* stuck here, too, I'd say that you clearly ran into the same brats."

"Yes."

She smiled. "Then it's very lucky that we ran into each other," she said. "Because neither of us could get out of limbo alone. But if we combine *my* magic with *your* science, I'm sure we can escape. And then we can help each other take over our own worlds."

"And fix those kids," Larry Lee added.

"Oh, yes." Lori Lee brushed her hair back so it was perfect. "Fixing those brats will be our *first* task. One I am looking forward to with great pleasure . . ."

To be continued in:
The Magical States of America #3
Double Disaster!

ABOUT THE AUTHOR

JOHN PEEL was born in Nottingham, England. He moved to Long Island, New York, to get married. He lives there still, writing novels full time, in a house filled with dogs. He and his wife, Nan, are very active in rescuing unwanted and abandoned miniature pinscher dogs. One recent pup was left tied to a tree in a Brooklyn park at midnight in December. He was saved from freezing and is now in a good home. (If you want to know what people are doing to help such abandoned pets, check out PetFinders at: *http://www.petfinder.org*, and you'll see what many volunteers all over the country are doing.)

Twice the Trouble! is his ninety-seventh book. Some of his others include *Star Trek* novels and series, such as *Diadem*, and *2099*.

Bruce Coville's

Magic Shop Books

THE MONSTER'S RING

Russell is shocked when he finds out what can happen after
three twists of the monster's ring.

JEREMY THATCHER, DRAGON HATCHER

She was just a little dragon until she grew, and grew, and grew.

JENNIFER MURDLEY'S TOAD

What do you do when your talking toad has an attitude?

THE SKULL OF TRUTH

It's talking, and it won't shut up!

A MINSTREL® BOOK

Published by Pocket Books

2054-01

William knows that Toad-in-a-Cage Castle has its share of
hidden mysteries. But in the midnight hours, he has to
wonder what could possibly be making those strange
moans echoing through the castle's halls.

Then one night he finds out . . . .

**"A shivery treat for readers, who will identify
with the stalwart William as he ferrets out the
castle's scary secrets and rights a long-existing
wrong." —*Booklist***

𝔊oblins
in the
𝔠astle

by Bruce Coville

Available from Minstrel® Books
Published by Pocket Books

1109-01

BRUCE COVILLE'S

The fascinating and hilarious adventures of
the world's first purple sixth grader!

I WAS A SIXTH GRADE ALIEN

THE ATTACK OF THE TWO-INCH TEACHER

I LOST MY GRANDFATHER'S BRAIN

PEANUT BUTTER LOVERBOY

ZOMBIES OF THE SCIENCE FAIR

DON'T FRY MY VEEBLAX!

TOO MANY ALIENS

SNATCHED FROM EARTH

THERE'S AN ALIEN IN MY BACKPACK

THE REVOLT OF THE MINATURE MUTANTS

THERE'S AN ALIEN IN MY UNDERWEAR

FAREWELL TO EARTH

A MINSTREL® BOOK
Published by Pocket Books   2304-07

Don't miss these books by

CAROL WALLACE AND BILL WALLACE

THE FLYING FLEA, CALLIE, AND ME

Callie was getting too old for the job, so the house people picked me to be a mouser. But I didn't plan on getting dive-bombed by a mockingbird building her nest...or adopting the baby who fell out. No joke! Flea—that's what I named her—couldn't even fly. She was pathetic. I had to help her. The first step was protecting Flea—and me—from the monster rats in the barn and Bullsnake under the woodpile. Next, Callie and I had to teach Flea to fly. After all, how could she stay up North with us when her bird family was flying to Florida? I know I'll miss my Flea. But she'll come back—after she's seen the world!

THAT FURBALL PUPPY AND ME

Here I am, a self-respecting kitten just trying to survive in a rat-eat-cat world, when the humans in my life start acting crazy. Something about the kids, and grandkids, coming to visit for Christmas. Mama accusing me of tearing up the presents. Noisy voices and grabby little hands. If the grandkids are bad, they're nothing compared to the gift the kids gave Mama for Christmas...a puppy! Dumb furball. Everybody is cooing over this yappy puppy who only wants to play. So I got him in trouble for tearing up the kitchen. Big deal. Problem is, I feel responsible. This puppy's headed for T*R*O*U*B*L*E. How can I save him? I can't even save myself!

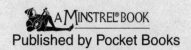

A MINSTREL® BOOK
Published by Pocket Books

2306-01